"Afraid to kiss me?"

Coreen whispered boldly.

Ted smiled faintly. "Maybe I am. You and I are explosive."

Her eyes were curious. "Isn't it always like that, for a man?"

His thumb slid over her chin and moved to tug at her soft lower lip. "Not for me," he confessed quietly. "I only feel this fever with you, Corrie," he whispered against her mouth, as he took it.

It was a mistake. He knew it the minute he felt her lips part beneath the ardent pressure of his mouth. He felt her shiver, and the world spun away....

LONG, TALL TEXANS

Back by popular demand! Bestselling author Diana Palmer continues her LONG, TALL TEXANS series featuring rugged heroes with their own special brand of loving!

Dear Reader,

It's time to celebrate! This month we are thrilled to present our 1000th Silhouette Romance novel—*Regan's Pride*, written by one of your most beloved authors, Diana Palmer. This poignant love story is also the latest addition to her ever-popular LONG TALL TEXANS.

But that's just the start of CELEBRATION 1000! Throughout April, May, June and July we'll be bringing you wonderful romances by authors you've loved for years— Debbie Macomber, Tracy Sinclair and Annette Broadrick. And so many of your new favorites—Suzanne Carey, Laurie Paige, Marie Ferrarella and Elizabeth August.

This month, look for *Marry Me Again* by Suzanne Carey, an intriguing tale of marriage to an irresistible stranger.

The FABULOUS FATHERS continue with *A Father's Promise* by Helen R. Myers. Left to care all alone for his infant son, Big John Paladin sets out to win back the woman he once wronged.

Each month of our celebration we'll also present an author who is brand-new to Silhouette Romance. In April, Sandra Steffen debuts with an enchanting story, *Child of Her Dreams*.

Be sure to look for *The Bachelor Cure*, a delightful love story from the popular Pepper Adams. And don't miss the madcap romantic reunion in *Romancing Cody* by Rena McKay.

We've planned CELEBRATION 1000! for you, our wonderful readers. So, stake out your favorite easy chair and put a Do Not Disturb sign on the door. And get ready to fall in love all over again with Silhouette Romance.

Happy reading!

Anne Canadeo
Senior Editor
Silhouette Romance

Please address questions and book requests to:
Reader Service
U.S.: P.O. Box 1325, Buffalo, NY 14269
Canadian: P.O. Box 1050, Niagara Falls, Ont. L2E 7G7

REGAN'S PRIDE
Diana Palmer

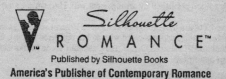

ROMANCE™

Published by Silhouette Books

America's Publisher of Contemporary Romance

For Babs

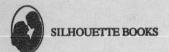 SILHOUETTE BOOKS

ISBN 0-373-19000-X

REGAN'S PRIDE

Copyright © 1994 by Diana Palmer

This edition published by arrangement with Harlequin Enterprises B.V.

® and TM are trademarks of Harlequin Enterprises B.V., used under
license. Trademarks indicated with ® are registered in the United States
Patent and Trademark Office, the Canadian Trade Marks Office and in
other countries.

Printed in U.S.A.

A Note from Diana Palmer

I can't begin to tell you what a great thrill it was for my book to be chosen as the 1000th Silhouette Romance title! Ted Regan has been around since the beginning of my Long, Tall Texans series, so he seemed to be the logical choice for this special contribution to the Romance series. I hope that you enjoy reading his story as much as I enjoyed writing it.

Thank you for your kindness to me over the years. And, in answer to all the wonderful letters I've received, I will be doing more books in my Long, Tall Texans series for Silhouette Romance. God bless.

All my best,

Diana Palmer

Chapter One

The tall, silver-haired man stood quietly apart from the rest of the mourners, his eyes narrowed and contemptuous on the slender, black-clad figure beside his sister. His cousin Barry was dead, and that woman was responsible. Not only had she tormented her husband of two years into alcoholism, but she'd allowed him to get behind the wheel of a car when he was drunk and he'd gone off a bridge to his death. And there she stood, four million dollars richer, without a single tear in her eyes. She looked completely untouchable—and Ted Regan knew that she had been, as far as her husband had been concerned.

His sister noticed his cold stare and left the widow's side to join him.

"Stop glaring at her. How can you be so unfeeling?" Sandy asked angrily. His sister had dark hair. At forty, he was fifteen years older than she, and prematurely gray. They shared the same pale blue eyes, though, and the same temper.

"Am I being unfeeling?" he asked with a careless smile, and raised his smoking cigarette to his mouth.

"You promised you were going to give that up," she reminded him.

He lifted a dark eyebrow. "I did. I only smoke when I'm under a lot of stress, and only outdoors."

"I wasn't worried about secondhand smoke. You're my brother, and I care about you," she said simply.

He smiled, and his hand touched her face briefly. "I'll try to quit. Again," he said wryly. He glanced at the widow with cold eyes. "She's a case, isn't she? I haven't seen a single tear. They were married for two years."

"Nobody knows what goes on inside a marriage, Ted," she reminded him quietly.

"I suppose not," he mused. "I've never wanted to marry anybody, but it seems to work out for a few people."

"Like the Ballengers here in Jacobsville," she agreed with a smile. "They go on forever. I envy them."

Ted wasn't going to touch that line with a pole. He drew on the cigarette, and his harsh gaze went back to the heavily veiled woman by the black limousine.

"Why the veil?" he asked coldly. "Is she afraid Barry's mother may wonder why there aren't any tears in her big blue eyes?"

"You're so cynical and harsh, Ted, it's no wonder to me that you've never married," she said with resignation. "I've heard people say that no woman in south Texas would be brave enough to take you on!"

"There's no woman in south Texas that I'd have," he countered.

"Least of all, Coreen Tarleton," she added for him, because the way he was looking at her best friend spoke volumes.

"She's even younger than you," he said curtly. "Twenty-four to my forty," he added quietly. "Years too young for me, even if I were interested. Which I am not," he added with a speaking glance.

"She isn't what you think," Sandy said.

"I'm glad you're loyal to the people you love, tidbit, but you're never going to convince me that the merry widow over there is grieving."

"You've always been unkind to her," Sandy said.

He stiffened. "She was a pest once."

Sandy didn't reply. She'd often thought that Ted had been in love for the first time in his life with Coreen, but he'd let the age difference stand between them. He was forty, but he had the physique of a man half that age, and the expensive dark suit he was wearing flattered it. He was a working millionaire. He never sat at a desk. He was slender and strong, and as handsome as the late cowboy star Randolph Scott. But he had no use for women now; not since Coreen had married.

"You're coming back to the house with us, aren't you?" Sandy asked after a minute. "They're reading the will after lunch."

"In a hurry, is she?" he asked icily.

"It was Barry's mother's idea, not hers," Sandy shot back angrily.

"No surprises there," he remarked, his blue eyes searching for Barry's small, elegant mother in her black designer suit. "Tina probably would enjoy dumping Coreen on the front lawn in her underwear."

"She does seem a little hostile."

Ted ground out the cigarette under the heel of his highly polished dress boot. "Is that a surprise?" he asked frankly. "Coreen killed her son."

"Ted!"

His blue eyes looked hard enough to cut diamond. "She never loved him," he told her. "She married him because her father had died and she had nothing, not even a house to live in. And then she spent two years teasing and taunting him and making him unhappy. He used to cry on my shoulder...."

"How? You never went near their house, except once, to visit for a few hours," she recalled. "You even refused to be best man at his wedding."

He averted his eyes. "He came to Victoria pretty often to see me," he said. "And he wasn't a stranger to a telephone. We had business dealings together. I heard all about Coreen from him," he added darkly. "She drove him to drink."

"Coreen is my friend," she responded. "Even if I believed that about her, it wouldn't matter. Friends accept the bad with the good."

He shrugged. "I wouldn't know. I don't have friends."

How well Sandy knew it, too. Ted didn't trust anyone that close, man or woman.

"You could make the gesture of giving her your condolences," she said finally.

He lifted an eyebrow. "Why should I give her sympathy when she doesn't care that her husband is dead?

Besides, I don't do a damned thing for the sake of appearances."

She made a sound in her throat and went back to Coreen.

The ride back to the redbrick mansion was short. Coreen was quiet. They were almost to the front door before she looked at Sandy and spoke.

"Ted was saying something about me, wasn't he?" she asked, her voice strained. Her face was very pale in its frame of short, straight black hair and her deep blue eyes were tragic.

Sandy grimaced. "Yes."

"You don't have to soft-pedal Ted's attitude to me," came the wistful reply. "I've known Ted ever since you and I became friends in college, remember?"

"Yes, I remember," Sandy agreed.

"Ted never liked me, even before I married his cousin." She didn't mention how she knew it, or that Ted had been the catalyst who caused her to rush headlong into a marriage that she hadn't even wanted.

"Ted doesn't want commitment. He plays the field," Sandy said evasively.

"His mother really affected him, didn't she?" Coreen knew about their childhood, because Sandy had told her.

"Yes, she did. He's been a rounder most of his life because of it," she added on a sigh. "I used to think he had a case on you, before you married," she added with a swift glance. "He was violent about you. He still is. Odd, wouldn't you say?"

Coreen didn't betray her thoughts by a single expression. She'd learned to hide her feelings very well. Barry had homed in on any sign of weakness or vulnerability.

She'd made the mistake once, only once, of talking about Ted, during the first weeks of her marriage to Barry. She hadn't realized until later that she'd given away her feelings for him. Barry had gotten drunk that night and hurt her badly. It had taught her to keep her deepest feelings carefully concealed.

"It will all be over soon," Sandy remarked.

"Will it?" Coreen asked quietly. Her long, elegant fingers were contracting on her black clutch bag.

"Why did Tina want the will read so quickly?" Sandy asked suddenly.

"Because she's sure that Barry left everything to her, including the house," she said quietly. "You know how opposed she was to our marriage. She'll have me out the front door by nightfall if the will did make her sole beneficiary. And I'll bet it did. It would be like Barry. Even when we were married, I had to live on a household allowance of a hundred dollars a week, and bills and groceries had to come out of that."

Her best friend stared at her. It had suddenly dawned on her that the dress Coreen was wearing wasn't a new one. In fact, it was several years out of style.

"I only have the clothes I bought before I married," Coreen said with ragged pride, avoiding her friend's eyes. "I've made do. It didn't matter."

All Sandy could think about was that Tina was wearing a new designer dress and driving a new Lincoln. "But, why? Why did he treat you that way?"

Coreen smiled sadly. "He had his reasons," she said evasively. "I don't care about the money," she added quietly. "I can type and I have the equivalent of an associate degree in sociology. I'll find a way to make a living."

"But Barry would have left you something, surely!"

She shook her head at Sandy's expression. "He hated me, didn't you know? He was used to women fawning all over him. He couldn't stand being anyone's second choice," she said enigmatically. "At least there won't be any more fear," she added with nightmarish memories in her eyes. "I'm so ashamed."

"Of what?"

"The relief I feel," she whispered, as if the car had ears. "It's over! It's finally over! I don't even care if people think I killed him." She shivered.

Sandy was curious, but she didn't pry. Coreen would tell her one day. Barry had done everything in his power to keep her from seeing Coreen. He didn't like anyone near his wife, not even another woman. At first, Sandy had thought it was obsessive love for Coreen that caused him to behave that way. But slowly it dawned on her that it was something much darker. Whatever it was, Coreen had kept to herself, despite Sandy's careful probing.

"It will be nice not to have to sneak around to have lunch with you once in a while," Sandy said.

Worried blue eyes met hers through the delicate lace veil. "You didn't tell Ted that we had to meet like that?"

"No. I haven't told Ted," was the reply. Sandy hesitated. "If you must know, Ted wouldn't let me talk about you at all."

The thin shoulders moved restlessly and the blue eyes went back to the window. "I see."

"I don't," Sandy muttered. "I don't understand him at all. And today I'm actually ashamed of the way he's acting."

"He loved Barry."

"Maybe he did, in his way, but he never tried to see your side of it. Barry wasn't the same with another man as he was with you. Barry bullied you, but most people don't try to bully Ted, if they've got any sense at all."

"Yes, I know."

The limousine stopped and the driver got out to open the door for them.

"Thanks, Henry," Coreen said gratefully.

Henry was in his fifties, an ex-military man with close-cropped gray hair and muscle. He'd been her salvation since he came to work for Barry six months ago. There had been gossip about that, and some people thought that Coreen was cuckolding her husband. Actually Henry had served a purpose that she couldn't tell anyone about.

"You're welcome, Mrs. Tarleton," Henry said gently.

Sandy went into the house with Coreen, noticing with curiosity that there seemed to be no maid, no butler, no household staff at all. In a house with eight bedrooms and bathrooms, that seemed odd.

Coreen saw the puzzled look on her friend's face. She took off her veiled hat and laid it on the hall table. "Barry fired all the staff except Henry. He tried to fire Henry, too, but I convinced him that he needed a chauffeur."

There was no reply.

Coreen turned and stared at Sandy levelly. "Do you think I'm sleeping with Henry?"

Sandy pursed her lips. "Not now that I've seen him," she replied with a twinkle in her eyes.

Coreen laughed, for the first time in days. She turned and led the way into the living room. "Sit down and I'll make a pot of coffee."

"You will not. I'll make it. You're the one who needs to rest. Have you slept at all?"

The shorter woman's shoulders lifted and fell. She was just five foot five in her stocking feet, for all her slenderness. Sandy, three inches taller, towered over her. "The nightmares won't stop," she confessed with a small twist of her lips.

"Did the doctor give you anything to make you sleep?"

"I don't take drugs."

"A sleeping pill when someone has died violently is hardly considered a drug."

"I don't care. I don't want to be out of control." She sat down. "Are you sure you don't want me to...?"

The front door opened and closed. There hadn't been a knock, and only one person considered himself privileged enough to just walk in. Coreen refused to look up as Ted entered the living room, loosening his tie as he came. He wasn't wearing his Stetson, or even the dress boots he usually favored. He looked elegant and strange in his expensive suit.

"I was just about to make coffee," Sandy said, giving him a warning look. "Want some?"

"Sure. A couple of leftover biscuits would be nice, too. I didn't stop for breakfast."

"I'll see what I can find to fix." Sandy didn't mention that it was odd no one had offered to bring food. It was an accepted tradition in most rural areas, and this was Jacobsville, Texas. It was a very close-knit community.

Ted didn't have any inhibitions about asking embarrassing questions. He sat down in the big armchair across from the burgundy velvet-covered sofa where Coreen was sitting.

"Why didn't anybody bring food?" he asked her bluntly. He smiled coldly. "Do your neighbors think you killed him, too?"

Coreen felt the nausea in the pit of her stomach. She swallowed it down and lifted cool blue eyes to his. She ignored the blatant insult. "We had no close neighbors, nor did we have any close friends. Barry didn't like people around us."

His expression tautened as he glared at her. "And you didn't like Barry around you," he said with soft venom. "He told me all about you, Coreen. Everything."

She could imagine the sort of things Barry had confided. He liked having people think she was frigid. She closed her eyes and rubbed at her forehead, where the beginnings of a headache were forming. "Don't you have a business to run?" she asked heavily. "Several businesses, in fact?"

He crossed one long leg over the other. "My favorite cousin is dead," he reminded her. "I'm here for the funeral."

"The funeral is over," she said pointedly.

"And you're four million dollars to the good. At least, until the will is read. Tina's on the way back from the cemetery."

"Urged on by you, no doubt," she said.

His eyebrows arched. "I didn't need to urge her."

The pain and torment of the past two years ate at her like acid. Her eyes were haunted. "No, of course you didn't."

She got up from the sofa, elegant in the expensive black dress that clung to her slender—too slender—body. He didn't like noticing how drawn she looked. He knew that she hadn't loved Barry; she certainly wasn't mourning him.

"Don't expect much," he said with a cold smile.

The accusation in his eyes hurt. "I didn't kill Barry," she said.

He stood up, too, slowly. "You let him get into a car and drive when he'd had five neat whiskeys." He nodded at her look of surprise. "I grew up in Jacobsville. I'm acquainted with most people who live here, and you know that Sandy and I have just moved back into the old homestead. Everybody's been talking about Barry's death. You were at a party and he wanted you to drive him home. You refused. So he went alone, and shot right off a bridge."

So that was how the gossips had twisted it. She stared at Ted without speaking. Sandy hadn't mentioned that they were coming home to Jacobsville. How was she going to survive living in the same town with Ted?

"No defense?" he challenged mockingly. "No excuses?"

"Why bother?" she returned wearily. "You wouldn't believe me."

"That's a fact." He stuck his hands into his pockets, aware of loud noises in the kitchen. Sandy, reminding him that she was still around.

Coreen folded her hands in front of her to keep them from trembling. Did he have to look at her with such cold accusation?

"Barry wrote to me two weeks ago. He said that he'd changed his will and that I was mentioned in it." He stared at her mockingly. "Didn't you know?"

She didn't. She only knew that Barry had changed the will. She knew nothing of what was in it.

"Tina's in it, too, I imagine," he continued with a smile so smug that it made her hands curl.

She was tired. Tired of the aftermath of the nightmare she'd been living, tired of his endless prodding. She pushed back her short hair with a heavy sigh. "Go away, Ted," she said miserably. "Please . . ."

She was dead on her feet. The ordeal had crushed her spirit. She felt tears threatening and she turned away to hide them, just as their betraying glitter began to show. She caught her toe in the rug and stumbled as she wheeled around. She gasped as she saw the floor coming up to meet her.

Incredibly he moved forward and caught her by the shoulders. He pulled her around and looked into her pale, drawn face. Then without a word, he slid his arms around her and stood holding her, gently, without passion.

"How did you manage that?" he asked, as if he thought she'd done it deliberately.

She hadn't. She was always tripping over her own feet these days. Tears stung her eyes as she stood rigidly in his hold, her heart breaking. He didn't know, couldn't know, how it had been.

"I didn't manage it," she whispered in a raw tone. "I tripped, and not because I couldn't wait to get your arms around me! I don't need anything from you!"

Her tone made him bristle with bad temper. "Not even my love?" he asked mockingly, at her ear. "You begged for it, once," he reminded her coldly.

She shivered. The memory, like most others of the past two years, wasn't that pleasant. She started to step back but his big hands flattened on her shoulder blades and held her against him. She was aware, too aware, of the clean scent of his whipcord lean body, of the rough sigh of his breath, the movement of his broad chest so close that the tips of her breasts almost touched it. Ted, she thought achingly. Ted!

Her hands were clenched against his chest, to keep them honest. She closed her eyes and ground her teeth together.

The hands on her back had become reluctantly caressing, and she felt his warm breath at the hair above her temple. He was so tall that she barely came up to his nose.

Under the warmth of his shirtfront, she could feel hard muscle and thick hair. He was offering her comfort, something she hadn't had in two long years. But he was like Barry, a strong, domineering man, and she was no longer the young woman who'd worshiped him. She knew what men were under their civilized veneer, and now she couldn't stand this close to a man without feeling threatened and afraid; Barry had made sure of it. She made a choked, involuntary sound as she felt Ted's hands contract around her upper arms. He was bruising her without even realizing it. Or did he realize it? Was he thinking of ways to punish her, ways that Barry hadn't gotten to?

Ted heard the pitiful sound she made, and the control he thought he had went into eclipse. "Oh, for God's sake," he groaned, and suddenly wrapped her up tight so that she was standing completely against him from head to toe. His tall body seemed to ripple with pleasure as he felt her against it.

Coreen shuddered. Two years ago, it would have been heaven to stand this close to Ted. But now, there were only vague memories of Ted and bitter, violent ones of Barry. Physical contact made her afraid now.

The tears came, and she stood rigidly in Ted's embrace and let them fall hotly to her cheeks as she gave in to the pain. The sobs shook her whole body. She cried for Barry, whom she never loved. She cried for herself, because Ted held her in contempt, and even if he hadn't, Barry had destroyed her as a woman. She wept until she was exhausted, drained.

Sandy stopped at the doorway, her eyes on Ted's expression as he bent over Coreen's dark head. Shocked, Sandy quickly made a noise to alert him to her presence, because she knew he wouldn't want anyone to see the look on his face in that one brief, unguarded moment.

"Coffee!" she announced brightly, and without looking directly at him.

Ted released Coreen slowly, producing a handkerchief that he pressed angrily into her trembling hands. She wouldn't look up at him. That registered, along with her rigid posture that hadn't relaxed even when she cried in his arms, and the deep ache inside him that holding her had created.

"Sit down, Corrie, and have a buttered biscuit," Sandy said as Ted moved quickly away and sat down again. "I found these wrapped up on the table."

"Mrs. Masterson came early this morning and made breakfast," Coreen recalled shakily. "I don't think I ate any."

"Tina said that she's staying at a motel," Ted remarked. He was furious at his own weakness. He hadn't meant to let it go that far.

She wiped her eyes and looked at him then. "She and I don't get along. She didn't want to stay here," she replied. "I did offer."

He averted his eyes to the cup of black coffee that Sandy handed him.

"You should take a few days to rest," Sandy told her friend. "Go down to the Caribbean or somewhere and get away from here."

"Why not?" Ted drawled, staring coldly at the widow. "You can afford it."

"Stop," Coreen said wildly, her eyes like saucers in her white face. "Stop it, can't you?"

"Ted, please!" Sandy added.

The sound of a car coming up the driveway diverted him. He got up and went to the door, refusing to look at Coreen again. His loss of control had shaken him.

"I can't stand this," Coreen whispered frantically. "He does nothing but try to get at me!"

"Barry said something to him," Sandy revealed curtly. "I don't know what. He mentioned at the cemetery that he'd seen him quite often and that Barry had told him things about you."

"Knowing Barry, he invented some of them to make himself look even more pitiful," Coreen said softly. "I was his scapegoat, his excuse for every terrible thing he did. He drank because of me, didn't you know?"

"He drank because he wanted to," Sandy corrected.

"You're the only person in Jacobsville who believes that," her friend said. She sipped her coffee, aware of voices in the hall, one deep and gentle, the other sharp and impatient.

"I thought that lawyer would be here by now," Tina Tarleton said irritably, stripping off her white gloves as she joined the women. She was resplendent in a black suit by Chanel and had on only the finest accessories to match.

"I imagine he had to go by his office and get the paperwork first," Coreen said.

Tina glared at her. "No doubt he'll be here soon. I'd start packing if I were you."

"I already have," Coreen said. "It didn't take long," she added enigmatically.

Another car came up. Sandy went to the hall window. "The lawyer," she announced, and went to open the door.

"Finally," Tina snapped. "It's about time!"

Coreen didn't reply. She was staring at the chair where Barry used to sit, remembering. Her eyes were suddenly haunted, almost afraid.

Ted glared at her from his own chair. So she felt guilty, did she? And well she should. He hoped her conscience hurt her. He hoped she never had another minute's peace.

She felt his glare and looked at him. His hands almost broke the arms of the chair he was occupying as he stared into her dead eyes with violence in his own.

The lawyer, a tall, graying gentleman, came into the room with Sandy and broke the spell. Coreen was ready to give thanks. She couldn't really understand why Ted should hate her so much over the death of a cousin he wasn't really that close to. But, then, he'd always hated her. Or at least, he'd given the appearance of hating her. He'd been hostile since that first time, two years ago, when he'd found himself forced into her company....

Chapter Two

Coreen had been friends with Sandy Regan for four
years, but she was in her second year of college before
she really got to know Ted Regan. She was helping her
father in his feed store in Jacobsville and Ted had come
in with the new foreman at his ranch to open an ac-
count.

In the past, he'd always done business with a rival
feed store, but it had just gone out of business. He was
forced to buy from Coreen's father, or drive to Victoria for supplies. He was courteous to Coreen, but not
overly friendly. That wasn't new. From the beginning of
her friendship with his sister, he'd been cool to her.

Coreen had found him fascinating from the first time
she'd looked into those pale eyes, when Sandy had introduced them. Ted had given her a long, careful ap-
praisal, and obviously found the sight of her offensive
because he absented himself immediately after the in-

troduction and thereafter maintained a careful distance whenever Coreen came out to the ranch.

Coreen wasn't hurt; she took it for granted that a sophisticated man like Ted wouldn't want to encourage her by being friendly. She'd been gangly and tomboyish in her jeans and sweatshirt and sneakers. Ted was almost a generation older, and already a millionaire. His name had been linked with some of the most beautiful and eligible women around Texas, even if his distaste for marriage was well-known.

But he noticed Coreen. Although it might have been reluctant on his part, his pale eyes followed her around the store every week while she filled his orders. But he came no closer than necessary.

As time went by, Coreen heard about him from Sandy and got to know him in a secondhand sort of way. Slowly she began to fall in love, until two years ago, he had become her whole life. He pretended not to see her interest, but it became more obvious as she fumbled and stammered when he came around the store.

It was inevitable that he would touch her from time to time as they passed paperwork back and forth, and suddenly it was like electricity between them. Once, she stood with her back to the counter and suddenly looked up into his eyes. He was standing so close that she could breathe in the very masculine scent of his cologne. He hadn't moved, hadn't blinked, and the intensity of the stare had made her knees weak. His gaze had dropped abruptly to her soft, pink mouth and her heartbeat had gone wild. She might be innocent, but even a novice could recognize the sort of desire that had flared unexpectedly in Ted's hard, lean face at that moment. It was the first time he'd ever really looked at her, she knew. It was as if, before, he'd forced himself not to notice her slender body and pretty face.

Her father's arrival had broken the spell, and Ted's expression had become one of self-contempt mingled with anger and something much more violent. He'd left the store at once.

Coreen had built dreams on that look they'd shared. As if Ted was caught in the same web, his trips to the feed store became more frequent and always, he watched her.

In her turn, she noticed that he usually came in on Wednesdays and on Saturdays, so she started dressing to the hilt on those days. Her slender, tomboyish figure could look elegant when she chose the right sort of clothes, and Ted didn't, or couldn't, hide his interest. His pale eyes followed her with visible hunger every time he came near her. The tension between them grew swiftly until one day things came to a head.

They were in the storeroom together, looking for a particular kind of bridle bit he wanted for his tack room. Coreen tripped over some coiled rope and Ted caught her easily, his reflexes honed by years of dangerous ranch work.

"Careful," he'd murmured at her forehead. "You could have pitched headfirst into those shovels."

"With my hard head, I'd never have felt it." She laughed, looking up at him. "I'm clumsy sometimes..."

The laughter had stopped when she saw his face. The lean hands holding her had brought her quite suddenly against the length of his body and secured her there. She could feel his chest move against her breasts when he breathed, and his breathing was as ragged as her own.

With a soft laugh full of self-contempt, he bent and brushed his open mouth roughly over her lips, teasing them with a skill that Coreen had never experienced. She stiffened, and he searched her eyes narrowly. Then he did it again, and this time she held her face up for him, poised like a sacrifice in his warm embrace.

"Do you know how old I am?" he asked against her mouth in a voice gone deep and gravelly with emotion.

"No."

"I'm thirty-eight," he murmured. "You're nearly twenty-two. I'm sixteen years your senior. We're almost a generation apart."

"I don't care...!" she began breathlessly.

His head lifted. "There's no future in it," he said mercilessly as he searched her face with quick, hard eyes. "You're infatuated and set on your first love affair, but it can't, it won't, be me. I'm long past the age of hand-holding and petting."

She stared at him uncomprehendingly. Her body was throbbing with emotion and she wanted nothing more than his mouth on hers.

"You aren't even listening," he chided huskily. His gaze fell to her soft mouth. "Do you know what you're inviting?" He drew her up on her tiptoes and his hard mouth closed slowly, expertly, on hers, teasing her lips apart with a steady insistent pressure that made her body feel swollen and shivery. She hesitated, frightened by it.

"No, you don't," he whispered, containing her instinctive withdrawal. "If I teach you nothing else, it's going to be that desire isn't a game."

One lean hand went to her nape, holding her head steady, and then his mouth began to torment hers in brief, rough, biting kisses. He aroused her so swiftly, so completely, that she pressed into him with a harsh whimper and clung, her legs trembling against his as her young body pleaded for relief from the torment that racked it.

She had no control, but Ted never lost his. Tempestuous seconds later, he lifted his mouth from hers slowly, inch by inch, his hands contracting around her upper arms as he eased her away from him and looked down into her shattered eyes.

She knew how she must look, with her swollen mouth still pleading for his kisses, her body trembling with the residue of what he'd aroused. She couldn't hide her reaction. But none of his showed in his face.

"Do you begin to see how dangerous it is?" he asked with unusual softness in his deep voice. "I could have you against the counter, right now. You're too shaken, too curious, to deny me, and I'm fairly human in my needs. I can see everything you feel, everything you want, in your face. You have no defense at all."

"But you...don't you...want me?" she stammered.

His face contorted for an instant. Then suddenly, all expression left his face. His hands contracted and one corner of his mouth pulled up. "I want a woman," he said mercilessly. "You're handy. That's all it is."

The revelation was shattering to her ego. "Oh. Oh, I...I see."

"I hope so. You're very obvious lately, Coreen. You hang around the ranch waiting for me, you dress up when I come into the feed store. It's flattering, but I don't want your juvenile attention or your misplaced infatuation. I'm sorry to be so blunt, but that's how it is. You aren't the kind of woman who attracts me. You have the body and the outlook of an adolescent."

She went scarlet. Had she been so obvious? She moved back from him, her arms crossing over her breasts. She was devastated.

His jaw tautened as he looked at her wounded expression, but he didn't recant. "Don't take it so hard," he said curtly. "You'll learn soon enough that we have to settle for what we can get in life. I'll send Billy for supplies from now on. And you'll find some excuse not to come out to the ranch to see Sandy. Won't you?"

She managed to nod. With a tight smile and threatening tears, she escaped the storeroom and somehow got through the rest of the day. Ted had paused at the front steps to look back at her, an expression of such pain on his face for an instant that she might have been forgiven for thinking he'd lied to her about his feelings. But later she decided that it must have been the sunlight reflecting off those cold blue eyes. He'd let her down hard, but if he couldn't return her feelings, maybe it was kinder in the long run.

From then on, Ted sent his foreman to buy supplies and never set foot in the feed store again. Coreen saw him occasionally on the streets of Jacobsville, the town being so small that it was impossible to avoid people forever. But she didn't look at him or speak to him. They went to the same cafeteria for lunch one day, totally by chance, and she left her coffee sitting untouched and went out the back way as he was being seated. Once she caught him watching her from across the street, his face faintly bemused, but he never came close. If he had, she'd have been gone like a shot. Perhaps he knew that. Her fragile pride had taken a hard knock.

She was eventually invited out to the ranch to visit Sandy, again, supposedly with Ted's blessing. Rather than make Sandy suspicious about her motives, she went, but first she made absolutely sure that Ted was out of town or at least away from the ranch. Sandy noticed and mentioned it, emphasizing that Ted had said it was perfectly all right for her to be there. Coreen wouldn't discuss it, no matter how much Sandy pried.

Once, after that, Ted came upon her unexpectedly at a social event. She'd gone with Sandy to a square dance to celebrate her twenty-second birthday. Neither of them had dates. Sandy hadn't mentioned that her brother had planned to go until they were already there. In the middle of a square dance, Coreen found herself passed from one partner to the other until she came face-to-face with a somber Ted. To his surprise, and everyone else's, she walked off the dance floor and went home.

Gossip ran rampant in Jacobsville after that, because it was the first time in memory that any woman had snubbed Ted Regan publicly. Her father found it curious and amusing. Sandy was devastated; but it was the last time she tried to play Cupid.

There was one social event that Coreen hadn't planned on attending, since Ted would certainly be there. Her father belonged to a gun club and Coreen had always gone with him to target practice and meetings. Ted was the club president.

Coreen had long since stopped going to the club, but when the annual dance came around, her father insisted that she attend. She didn't want to. Sandy had already told her in a puzzled way that Ted went wild every time Coreen's name was mentioned since that square dance. She probably wondered if it was something more than having Coreen snub him at the dance, but she was too polite to ask.

Ted's venomous glare when he saw her at the gun club party was unsettling. She was wearing a sequined silver dress with spaghetti straps and a low V-neckline, with silver high heels dyed to match it. Her black hair had been waist-length at the time, and it was in a complicated coiffure with tiny wisps curling around her oval face. She looked devastating and the other men in attendance paid her compliments and danced with her. Ted danced with no one. He nursed a whiskey soda on the sidelines, talked to the other men present and glared at Coreen.

He seemed angry out of all proportion to her attendance. Ted had been wearing a dinner jacket with a ruffled white shirt and diamond-and-gold cuff links, and expensive black slacks. There was a red carnation in his lapel. The unattached women fell over themselves trying to attract him, but he ignored them. And then, incredibly, Ted had taken her by the hand, without asking if she wanted to dance, and pulled her into his arms.

Her heart had beaten her breathless while they slowly circled the floor. This was more than a duty dance, because his pale blue eyes were narrowed with anger. As the lights lowered, he'd maneuvered her to the side door and out into the moonlit darkness. There, he'd all but thrown her back against the wall.

"Why did you come tonight?" he said tersely. His blue eyes flared like matches as he stared at her in the light from the inside.

"Not because of you," she began quickly, ready to explain that she hadn't wanted to attend in the first place, but her well-meaning father had insisted. He didn't know about her crush on Ted. He wanted her to meet some eligible men.

"No?" Ted had challenged. His cold gaze had wandered over her and his lids came down to cover the expression in them. "You want me. Your eyes tell me so every time you look at me. You can walk away from dances or refuse to speak to me on the street, but you're only fooling yourself if you think it doesn't show!"

Her dark blue eyes had glittered up at him with temper. "You're very conceited!"

He'd paused to light a cigarette, but as his eyes swept over her, he suddenly tossed it off the porch into the sand and stepped forward. "It isn't conceit." He bit off the words, jerking her into his body.

His hand caught her by the nape and held her face poised for the downward descent of his. Her missed breath was audible.

The look in her eyes made him hesitate. Despite all her denials, she looked as if he was offering her heaven. Her breath came in sharp little jerks that were audible.

That excited him. His free hand went to her bodice and spread at the top of the V-neckline against her soft, warm skin. She gasped and as her mouth opened, his lips parted and settled on it. Her faint, anguished moan sent him spinning right off the edge of the world.

He forgot her age and his conscience the second he felt her soft, warm mouth tremble before it began to answer the insistent pressure of his own. He remembered too well the first taste he'd had of her, because his dreams had tormented him ever since. He'd thought he was imagining the pleasure he'd had with her, but he wasn't. The reality was just as devastating as the memory, and he couldn't help himself.

The hand behind her head contracted, bringing her mouth in to closer contact with his, and his free hand slid uninhibitedly down inside her bodice to cover one small, hard-tipped breast.

She protested, but not strongly enough to deter him. The feel of that big, warm, callused hand so intimately on her skin made her tremble with new sensations. She clung to his arms while he tasted and touched. She barely noticed the tiny strap being eased down her arm, or the slow relinquishing of her mouth, until she felt his mouth slide down her throat, over her collarbone and finally onto the warm silkiness of her breast.

She made a harsh sound and her nails bit into his arms.

"Don't cry out," he whispered at her breast. "Bite back those exciting little cries or we're going to become the evening's entertainment." His hand lifted her gently to his waiting mouth. He took the hard nipple inside and slowly, tenderly, began to suckle her.

She wept noiselessly at the ecstasy of his touch, clinging, shivering, as his mouth pleasured her. When it lifted, she hung against him, yielded, waiting, her eyes half-closed and misty with arousal. He looked at her face for one long instant before he pushed the other strap down her arm and watched the silky material fall to her waist. His hands arched her and his head bent. He hesitated just long enough to fill his eyes with the

exquisite sight of her bare breasts before he took her
inside his hungry mouth, and for a few brief, incandes-
cent seconds, she flew among the stars with him.

She slumped against him when he finally managed to
stop. She heard him dragging in long, ragged breaths
while he lifted her bodice back into place and eased the
shoulder straps up to support it. Then he held her while
she shivered.

"Am I the first?" he asked roughly.

"Yes." She couldn't have lied to him. She was too
weak.

The callused hands at her back contracted bruisingly
for a minute. He cursed under his breath, furiously.
"This is wrong. Wrong!" He bit off the words. "You're
so young...!"

Her soft cheek nuzzled against his throat. "I love
you," she whispered. "I love you more than my own
life."

"Stop it!" He pushed her away. His eyes were
frightening, glittery and dangerous. He moved back, his
face rigid with controlled passion, tormented. "I don't
want your love!"

She looked at him sadly, her big blue eyes soft and
gentle and vulnerable. "I know," she said.

His face corded until it looked like a mask over the
lean framework of his cheekbones. His fists clenched at
his side. "Stay away from me, Coreen," he said huskily. "I have nothing to give you. Nothing at all."

"I know that, too," she said, her voice calm even as
her legs trembled under her. At that moment, he looked
capable of the worst kind of violence. "You won't believe me, but I only came tonight because my father
wanted me to."

His face looked drawn, older. His eyes were like a rainy day, full of storms. "Don't build any dreams on what just happened. It was only sex," he said bluntly. "That's all it was, just a flash of sexual need that got loose for a minute. I'll never marry, and love isn't in my vocabulary."

"Because you won't let it be," she said quietly.

"Leave it alone, Coreen," he returned coldly.

She felt the chill, as she hadn't before. He was as unapproachable now as stone. The song that was playing inside suddenly caught her attention and she laughed a little nervously. "'Thanks for the Memory'." She identified it, and thought how appropriate it was.

"Don't kid yourself that this was any romantic interlude," he said with brutal honesty as he fought for breath. "You're just a kid...little more than a stick figure with two marbles for breasts. Now go away. Get out of my life and stay out!"

He'd walked off and left her out there. It was a summer night and warm. Coreen, wounded to the heart by that parting shot, had gone to her father's car and sat down in it. She hadn't gone back inside even when her father came out and asked what was wrong. A headache, she'd told him. He'd seen her leave with Ted, and he knew by the look on her face that she was hurt. He made their excuses and took her home.

Coreen had never gone to another gun club meeting or accepted another invitation from Sandy to come out to the ranch and ride horses. And on the rare occasions when Ted came into the store, she'd made herself scarce. She couldn't even meet his eyes, ashamed of her own lack of control and his biting comment about her body. For a man who thought she was too small-breasted, he certainly hadn't been reticent about touching her there, she thought. She knew so little about men, though, perhaps he meant the whole thing as a punishment. But if that had been so, why had his hands trembled?

Eventually she'd come to grips with it. She'd put Ted into a compartment of her past and locked him up, and she'd pretended that the night of the dance had never happened. Then her father had a heart attack and became an invalid. It was up to Coreen to run the business and she wasn't doing very well. That was when Barry had come into her life. Coreen and her father had been forced to put the feed store on the market and Barry had liked the prospect of owning it. He'd also liked the looks of Coreen, and suddenly made himself indispensable to her and her father. Anything they needed, he'd get them, despite her pride and protests.

He was always around, offering comfort and soft kisses to Coreen, who was upset about the doctor's prognosis, and hungry for a little kindness. Ted's behavior had killed something vulnerable in her. Barry's attention was a soothing balm to her wounds.

Ted had heard that his favorite cousin, Barry, was seeing a lot of Coreen. Ted stopped by often to see her father, and he watched her now, in an intense, disturbing way. He was gentle, almost hesitant, when he spoke to her. But Coreen had learned her lesson. She was distant and barely polite, so remote that they might have been strangers. When he came close, she moved away. That had stopped him in his tracks the first time it happened.

After that, he became cruel with her, at a time when she needed tenderness desperately. He began to taunt her about Barry, out of her father's hearing, mocking her for trying to entice his rich cousin to take care of her. Everyone knew that the feed store was about to go bankrupt because of the neglect of her sick father and his mounting medical bills.

The taunts frightened her. She knew how desperate their situation was becoming, and she daren't ask Ted for help in his present mood. Ironically his attitude pushed her further into Barry's waiting arms. Her vulnerability appealed to Barry. He took over, assuming the debts and taking the load from Coreen's shoulders.

The night her father died, Barry took charge of everything, paid all the expenses and proposed marriage to Coreen. She was confused and frightened, and when Ted came by the house to pay his respects, Barry wouldn't let him near her. Ted left in a furious mood and Barry convinced Coreen that his cousin hadn't wanted to speak to her, anyway.

Barry was beside her every minute at the funeral, keeping her away from Ted's suspicious, concerned gaze and making sure he had not a minute alone with her. The same day, he presented her with a marriage license and coaxed her into taking a blood test.

Ted left on a European business trip just after he refused Barry's invitation to be best man at the wedding. Ted's face when Barry made the announcement was indescribable. He looked at Coreen with eyes so terrible that she trembled and dropped her own. He strode out without a word to her and got on a plane the same day. It was confirmation, if Coreen needed it, that Ted didn't care what she did with her life as long as it didn't involve him. She might as well marry Barry as anyone, she decided, since she couldn't have the one man she loved.

But she was naive about the demands of marriage, and especially about the man Barry really was behind his social mask. Coreen lived in agony after her marriage. Barry knew nothing of tenderness and he was incapable of any normal method of satisfaction in bed. He had abnormal ways of fulfillment that hurt her and his cruelty wore away her confidence and her self-esteem until she became clumsy and withdrawn. Ted didn't come near them and Sandy's invitations were ignored by Barry. He all but broke up her friendship with Sandy. Not that it wouldn't have been broken up, anyway. Ted moved to Victoria and took Sandy with him, keeping the old Regan homestead for a holiday house and turning over the management of his cattle ranch to a man named Emmett Deverell.

Barry had known how Coreen felt about Ted. Eventually Ted became the best weapon in his arsenal, his favorite way of asserting his power over Coreen by taunting her about the man who didn't want her. They'd been married just a year when Ted finally accepted Barry's invitation to visit them in Jacobsville. Coreen hadn't expected Ted to come, but he had.

By that time, Coreen was more afraid of Barry than she'd ever dreamed she could be. He was impotent and he made intimacy degrading, a disgusting ordeal that made her physically sick. When he drank, which became a regular thing after their marriage, he became even more brutal. He blamed her for his impotence, he blamed her infatuation for Ted and harped on it all the time until finally she stiffened whenever she heard Ted's name. She tried to leave him several times, but a man of such wealth had his own ways of finding her and dealing with her, and with anyone who tried to help her. In the end she gave up trying, for fear of causing a tragedy. When he turned to other women, it was almost a relief. For a long time, he left her alone and she had peace, although she wondered if he was impotent with his lovers. But he began to taunt her again, after he'd run into Ted at a business conference. And he'd invited Ted to visit them in Jacobsville.

Ted had watched her covertly during that brief visit, as if something puzzled him. She was jumpy and nervous, and when Barry asked her for anything, she almost ran to get it.

"See?" Barry had laughed. "Isn't she the perfect little homemaker? That's my girl."

Ted hadn't laughed. He'd noticed the harried, hunted expression on Coreen's face and the pitiful thinness of her body. He'd also noticed the full liquor cabinet and remarked on it, because everyone knew that it was Tina's house that Barry and Coreen were staying in, and that Tina detested liquor.

"Oh, a swallow of alcohol doesn't hurt, and Coreen likes her gin, don't you, honey?" he teased.

Coreen kept her eyes hidden. "Of course," she lied. He'd already warned her about what would happen if she didn't go along with anything he said. He'd been even more explicit about the consequences if she so much as looked longingly at Ted. He'd invited his cousin to torment Coreen, and it was working. He was in a better humor than he'd enjoyed in months.

"Get us a drink. What will you have, Ted?"

The older man declined and and he didn't stay long. Ted had never come back to visit after that. Barry met his cousin occasionally and he enjoyed telling Coreen how sorry Ted felt for him. She knew that Barry was telling him lies about her, but she was too afraid to ask what they were.

Her life had become almost meaningless. It didn't help that her earlier clumsiness had been magnified tenfold. She was forever falling into flowerpots or tripping over throw rugs. Barry made it worse by constantly calling attention to it, chiding her and calling her names. Eventually she didn't react anymore. Her self-esteem was so low that it no longer seemed important to defend herself. She tried to run away. But he always found her...

He mentioned once how his mother, Tina, had controlled him all his life. Perhaps his weakness stemmed from her dominance and the lack of a father. His drinking grew worse. There were other women, scores of them, and in between he was cruel to Coreen, in bed and out of it. He was no longer discreet with his affairs. But he was less interested in tormenting Coreen as well. Until that card came from Sandy on Coreen's birthday, the day before the tragic accident that had killed Barry. It had Ted's signature on it, too, a shocking addition, and Barry had gone crazy at the sight of it. He'd gotten drunk and that night he'd held Coreen down on the sofa with a knife at her throat and threatened to cut her up....

A sudden buzz of conversation brought Coreen back to the present. Shivering from the memory, she focused her eyes on the big oak desk where the lawyer was sitting and realized that he was almost through reading the will.

"That does it, I'm afraid," he concluded, peering over his small glasses at them. "Everything goes to his mother. The one exception is the stallion he willed to his cousin, Ted Regan. And a legacy of one hundred thousand dollars is to be left to Mrs. Barry Tarleton, under the administration of Ted Regan, to be held in trust for her until she reaches the age of twenty-five. Are there any questions?"

Ted was scowling as he looked at Coreen, but there was no shock or surprise on her face. There was only stiff resignation and a frightening calmness.

Tina got to her feet. She glanced at Coreen coldly. "I'll give you a little while to get out of the house. Just to stem any further gossip, you understand, not out of any regard. I blame you for what happened to my son. I always will." She turned and left the room, her expression foreboding.

Coreen didn't reply. She stared at her hands in her lap. She couldn't look at Ted. She was homeless, and Ted controlled the only money she had. She could imagine that she'd have to go on her knees to him to get a new pair of stockings. She was going to have to get a job, quick.

"She could have waited until tomorrow," Sandy muttered to Ted when they were back outside, watching Tina climb into the Lincoln.

"Why did he do that?" Ted asked with open puzzlement. "For God's sake, he was worth millions! He's involved me in it, and she'll have literally nothing for another year, until she turns twenty-five! She'll even have to ask me for gas money!"

Sandy glanced at him with faint surprise at the concern he'd betrayed for Coreen. "She'll cope. She knew

Barry wasn't leaving her much. She's prepared. She said it didn't matter."

"Hell, of course it matters! Someone needs to talk some sense into her! She could sue for a widow's allowance."

"I doubt that she will. Money was never one of her priorities, or didn't you know?"

He didn't reply. His eyes were narrow and introspective.

"She looks odd, did you notice?" Sandy asked worriedly. "Really odd. I hope she isn't going to do anything foolish."

"Let's go," Ted said as he got in behind the steering wheel, and he sounded bitter. "I want to talk to that lawyer before we go home."

Sandy frowned as she looked at him. She was worried, but it wasn't about Coreen's money problems, or the will. Coreen was hopelessly clumsy since she'd married Barry. She said that she liked to skydive and go up in sailplanes, especially when she was upset, because she said it relaxed her. But she'd related tales of some of the craziest accidents Sandy had ever heard of. Sometimes she thought that Barry had programmed Coreen to be accident-prone. The few times early in their marriage that she'd seen her friend, before Barry had cut her out of Coreen's life, he'd enjoyed embarrassing Coreen about her clumsiness.

Ted didn't know about the accidents. Until the funeral, he'd walked away every time Sandy even mentioned Coreen, almost as if it hurt him to talk about her. He had the strangest attitude about her friend. He didn't care much for women, she knew, but the way he treated Coreen was intriguing. And the most curious thing had been the way he'd looked, holding Coreen in the living room earlier. The expression on his face had been one of torment, not hatred.

She was never going to understand her brother, she thought. The violence of his reaction to Coreen was completely at odds with the tenderness he'd shown her. Perhaps he did care, in some way, and simply didn't realize it.

Sandy insisted on staying with Coreen overnight, and she offered her best friend the sanctuary of the ranch until she found a place to live. Coreen refused bluntly, put off by even the thought of having to look at Ted over coffee every morning.

Coreen got her friend away the next morning, after a long and sleepless night blaming herself and remembering Ted's accusation of the day before.

"We're just getting moved in. Remember, Ted leased the place, along with the cattle farm, and we moved to Victoria about the time you married Barry. Ted's away a lot now, over at our cattle farm on the outskirts of Jacobsville, that Emmett Deverell and his family operate for him. We're going to have thoroughbred horses at our place and some nice saddle mounts. We can go riding like we used to. Won't you come with me? I'll work it out with Ted," Sandy pleaded.

"And let Ted drive me into a nervous breakdown?" came the brittle laugh. "No, thanks. He hates me. I didn't realize how much until yesterday. He would rather it had been me than Barry, didn't you see? He thinks I'm a murderess...!"

Sandy hugged her shaken friend close. "My brother is an idiot!" she said angrily. "Listen, he's not as brutal as he seems when you get to know him, really he isn't.''

"He's never been anything except cruel to me," Coreen replied, subdued. She pulled away. "Tell him to do whatever he likes with the trust, I won't need it. I can take care of myself. Be happy, Sandy. You've got a great career with that computer company, even a part interest. Make your mark in the world, and think of me once in a while. Try to remember all the good times, won't you?''

Sandy felt a chill run up her spine. Coreen had that restless look about her, all over again. There had been two bad accidents over the years because of Coreen's passion for flying and skydiving: a broken leg and two cracked ribs. Sandy had gone to see her in the hospital and Barry had been always in residence, refusing to let Coreen talk much about how the accidents had happened.

"Please be careful. You really are a little accident-prone," she began.

Coreen shivered. "Not really," she said. "Not anymore. Anyway, the people I skydive with watch out for me. I'll get better. I'm not suicidal, you know," she chided gently, and watched her friend blush. "I wouldn't kill myself over Ted's bad opinion of me. I wouldn't give him the satisfaction."

"Ted wouldn't want to see you hurt," Sandy said gently.

"Of course not," she said placatingly. "Now, go home. You've got a life of your own, although I really appreciate having you here. I needed you."

"Ted came voluntarily," she said pointedly. "I didn't ask him to."

Coreen's blue eyes darkened with pain. "He came to make me pay for hurting Barry," she said. "He's always found ways to make me pay, even for trying to care about him."

"You know why Ted won't let anyone close," Sandy said quietly. "Our mother was much younger than Dad. She ran away with another man when I was just a kid. Dad took it real hard. He gave Ted a vicious distrust of women, and I was the scapegoat until he died. Ted's kind to me, and he likes pretty women, but he wants no part of marriage."

"I noticed."

Sandy watched her closely. "He changed when you married. For the past two years, he's been a stranger. After he came back from that visit with you and Barry, he took off for Canada and stayed up there for a month and then he moved us to Victoria. He couldn't bear to talk about you."

"God knows why, I never did anything to him," Coreen said. "He knew Barry wanted to marry me and he thought I was after Barry's money, but he never tried to stop us."

Sandy let it drop, but not willingly. "Send me a postcard from wherever you move. I'll phone you then," she suggested. "We could meet somewhere for lunch."

Coreen's eyes were distracted. "Of course." She glanced at Sandy. "The birthday card..."

"Surprised, were you?" Sandy asked. "So was I. Ted had just talked to Barry. A day or two later, he saw a photograph of you and Barry in the Jacobsville paper he got in Victoria. He became very quiet when he saw it. You weren't smiling and you looked...fragile."

Coreen remembered the photograph. She and Barry had been at a charity banquet and he'd been drinking heavily—much more so than usual. She'd been at the end of her rope when the photographer caught them.

"Then Ted remembered that your birthday was up-coming," Sandy continued, "and he picked out a card to send you. For a man who hates you, he's amazingly contradictory, isn't he?"

She wondered at Ted's motives. Had he known how jealous Barry was of him? Had he done it to cause trouble? She couldn't bear to believe that he had. It was the card that had provoked Barry to threaten her that last night. Had it only been a week ago? She shivered mentally. She hugged Sandy and watched the other woman leave. When the car was out of sight, she picked up the telephone receiver and dialed.

"Hello, Randy?" she asked with a bright laugh. "When's the next jump? Tomorrow? Well, count me in. No, I'm not afraid of storms. It probably won't even be cloudy, you know how often they miss the forecast. Besides, I need a diversion. I'll see you out at the air-field at eight."

"Sure thing, lovely" came the teasing reply. She put the phone down and went to make sure her borrowed skydiving outfit was clean. She wouldn't think about getting out of the house right now. Tomorrow after-noon would be soon enough to start searching for an apartment and a job.

It was overcast, but not enough to deter the enthusi-astic crowd of jumpers. The jump from the plane was exhilarating, and even the sting from the faint pull of the stitches below her collarbone didn't detract from the pleasure of free-fall. Coreen had always loved the feeling she got from it. Earthbound people would never experience the rush of adrenaline that came from danger, the surge of emotion that rivaled the greatest pleasure she'd ever known—an unexpected glimpse of Ted Regan's face.

She pulled the cords to turn the parachute, looking for her mark below. Two other skydivers were heading down below her. But a gust of wind began to move her in a direction she didn't want to go, and when she looked up, she saw a gigantic thunderhead and a streak of lightning.

It was all she could do not to panic, and in her frantic haste to get her parachute going in the right direction, she overcontrolled it.

She was headed for a group of power lines. She'd read about ballooners who went into those electrical lines and didn't live to tell about it. She could see herself hitting them, see the sparks.

With a helpless cry as the thunder echoed around her, she jerked on the cord and moved her body, trying to force the stubborn 'chute to ignore the wind and bend to her will.

It was a losing battle, and she knew it. But she had nerve, and she wasn't going to give up until the last minute. The lightning forked past her and she closed her eyes, gritted her teeth and tried again to change direction.

The power lines were coming up. She was almost on them. She pulled her legs up with bent knees and jerked the 'chute. Her feet almost touched them, almost... but another gust of wind picked her up and moved her just a few inches, just enough to spare her landing on those innocent-looking black cables.

She let out a heavy sigh of relief. Rain had started to fall. She closed her eyes and through the thunder and lightning, she gave a prayer of thanks.

When she opened her eyes again, aware of the terrible darkness all around her as the unpredicted storm blew in, she saw what her fear had caused her to miss just minutes ago. There was a line of trees ahead, a thick conglomeration of pines and a few deciduous trees. They were right in the way. There was no cleared field, no place for her to land. She was going to go into those trees.

What if she landed in the very top of one? Would it take her weight, or would she fall to her death? And what about that huge oak? If she got caught in those leafy limbs, she could still be there when the first frost came!

The thought would have amused her once, but now she was too bent on survival to make jokes.

She didn't try to change direction. There was no use. Lightning streaked past her and hit one of the trees, smoke rising from it.

She thought that this was going to make an interesting addition to the obituary column, but at least she wouldn't go out in any dull manner.

She allowed herself one last thought, of Ted Regan's face when he read about it. She hoped that whoever planned her funeral wouldn't ruin it by letting Ted stand over her and make nasty remarks about her character.

The trees were coming closer. She could see the branches individually now, and with a sense of resignation, she let her body relax. If the fall didn't get her, the lightning probably would. She'd chosen her fate, and here it was.

It hadn't been a suicide attempt, although people would probably think so. She'd only wanted the freedom of the sky while she tried to come to grips with the rest of her life. She'd wanted to forget Ted's accusations and the cold way he'd looked at her.

What she remembered, though, was the rough, hungry clasp of his arms around her. Had he felt pity, for those few seconds when his embrace had bruised her? Or had it been a reflex action, the natural reaction of a man to having a woman in his arms? She'd never know.

She could picture his blue eyes and feel his mouth on hers, all those long years ago. She closed her own, waiting for death to come up and claim her. Her last conscious thought was that in whatever realm she progressed to, perhaps she could forget the one man she'd ever loved. And once she was gone, perhaps Ted could forgive her for everything he thought she'd done.

The impact was sudden, and surprisingly without pain. She felt the roughness of leaves and limbs and a hard, rough blow to her head. And then she felt nothing at all.

Chapter Three

Ted Regan had been sitting at his desk trying to make sense of a new prospectus. Sandy had only just gone out the door, after spending the night at the ranch. Suddenly, the front door was opened with force and his sister came running back in, red-faced and shaking.

"What is it?" he asked quickly, putting the papers aside.

"It's Corrie." She choked. Tears were running down her cheeks. "It was on the radio...she's been in a terrible accident!"

His heart stopped, started and ran away. He jerked out of his chair and took her by the arms. It wasn't pity for her that motivated him; it was the horror that made him go cold. "Is she dead?" She couldn't answer and he actually shook her. "Tell me! Is she all right?"

His white, desperate face shocked her into speech. "She was taken to the Jacobsville General emergency room." She choked out the words. "The radio said she was skydiving and fell into some trees or power lines or something. They don't know her condition."

He didn't stop to get his hat. He shepherded her out the door at a dead run.

Later, he didn't even remember the ride to the hospital. He marched straight to the desk, demanding to know how Coreen was and where she was. The woman clerk didn't try to deny him the information. She told him at once.

He walked straight into the recovery room, despite loud objections from a nurse.

Coreen was lying on a stretcher there, clad in a faded hospital gown. There were cuts and bruises all over her face and arms, and she was asleep.

"How is she?" he demanded.

The middle-aged nurse who was checking her vital signs nodded. "She'll be fine," she told him. "Dr. Burns can tell you anything you want to know. You're a relative?"

Technically he was, he supposed. If he said no, they wouldn't let him near her. "Yes," he said.

"Dr. Burns?" the nurse called to a green-gowned man outside the door. He excused himself from the doctor to whom he was speaking and came into the recovery room.

"This gentleman is a relative of Mrs. Tarleton."

Ted introduced himself and the doctor shook his hand warmly.

"I hope you know how much we all appreciate the pediatric critical care unit you funded here, Mr. Regan," the doctor said, and the nurse became flustered as she realized who their distinguished visitor was.

"It was my pleasure. How's Corrie?" he asked, nodding toward the pale woman on the bed.

"Minor concussion, a cracked rib and a burst appendix. We've repaired the damage, but someone should tell her not to skydive during thunderstorms," he said frankly. "This is her second close call in as many months. And we won't even go into the damage she sustained in the glider crash or her most recent brush with a sheet of tin..."

Ted went very still. "What glider crash?"

Dr. Burns lifted an eyebrow. "You said you were a relative?"

"Distant," he confessed. "Her husband was buried yesterday."

"Yes, I know."

"I'm from Victoria. I've just moved back here, into my grandfather's house."

"Oh, yes, the old Regan homeplace."

"The same," Ted continued. "I'd lost touch with Barry in the past few weeks, but we were cousins and fairly close. Funny, he never told me about any of Corrie's mishaps."

"That's surprising," the doctor said coolly, a sentiment that Ted could have seconded. He glanced down at Coreen's still form. "She's got two left feet. Her husband told me that a woman friend of Coreen's let her take up the glider and she flew it too close to the trees. Good thing it was insured. She needs to be watched. And I mean watched, until she's past this latest trauma. Then I'd strongly suggest some counseling. Nobody has so many accidents without an underlying cause. Perhaps she's running from something. Running scared."

Ted thought about that later when he and Sandy were drinking black coffee in the waiting room, waiting for them to move Corrie down into a private room. She was conscious, but barely out from under the anesthetic.

"Did you know that she'd had this sort of accident before?" Ted asked his sister.

She nodded. "I went to see her in the hospital. Or tried to. Barry didn't like it that I was there, and he wouldn't let me do more than wish her a speedy recovery. He kept everyone away from her, even then."

"Why didn't you say anything?"

"You didn't want to know, Ted," she replied honestly. "You hate Corrie. That was the last thing she said to me before I left, and there was a look in her eyes..." She grimaced. "She said something about my trying to remember the good times she and I had. It was an odd way of putting it, and I was afraid then that she planned to go up. She loves skydiving, but she's clumsy."

"I only remember Coreen ever being clumsy one time before she married," he said curtly. "How long has she been acting this way?"

She looked at him levelly. "Since about a month after she married Barry... about the same time he decided that Corrie and I shouldn't spend so much time together."

He was shocked. His white face told its own story, added to the way he was smoking. He wondered if his attitude at the funeral had driven Corrie into that airplane. Had he made her feel so much guilt that she couldn't even live with it? He hadn't really meant to, but he'd been fond of his young cousin, who'd always looked to him for advice and support, even above that of his own parents. And Coreen had let Barry drive drunk. That was the thing that haunted him. It was as if she'd condemned him to death.

"Well, I'll go over to the house in a day or so and have Henry open it up for me, so that I can get her clothes and things," Sandy said heavily. She finished her coffee. "Tina will probably have the locks changed soon and Corrie will have no place to go at all. I'll take her up to the apartment in Victoria with me...."

"We'll bring her to the ranch," Ted said firmly. "We can watch her, without letting her know that we are."

Sandy searched his face. "You won't be cruel to her?"

His jaw tautened. "I'll keep out of her way," he said, angry at the implication that he could hurt her now, when she could have been killed. His blue eyes impaled her. "That should please her."

He got up and moved down the corridor. Sandy stared after him with open curiosity.

Coreen was lying quietly in bed, feeling the bruises and cuts and breaks as if they were living things. The door opened and a familiar man walked in.

"Hello," she said groggily, and without smiling. "Did you come to gloat? Sorry to disappoint you, but one funeral is all you get this week."

He put his hands into his pockets and stood over her. Bravado, he concluded when he saw the faint fear in her eyes that underlaid the anger.

"How are you?" he asked.

She put a hand to her bruised forehead. "Tired," she said flatly.

"Jumping out of airplanes," he said with disgust, his eyes flaring at her. "In a damned thunderstorm! You haven't grown up at all."

Her dark blue eyes stared into his pale ones with weary resignation. "Leave me alone, Ted," she said in a drained voice. "I can't fight you right now."

He moved closer to the bed, his heart contracting at the sight of her lying there that way. "You little fool!" he said huskily. Suddenly he bent, one lean hand resting beside her head on the pillow, and his mouth covered hers so unexpectedly that she flinched.

He felt her involuntary movement and quickly lifted his lips from hers. His eyes stabbed into her own. He didn't know what he'd expected, but her rigid posture surprised him.

"That's new," he said, frowning absently.

She couldn't breathe. "Don't do that," she whispered.

"Why not?" he asked angrily. His chest rose and fell raggedly. "You wanted it once. Your eyes begged me for it every time you looked at me. But you don't feel that way now, do you? Did you know that Barry cried when he told me how frigid you were, that you wouldn't let him touch you... Corrie!"

She was crying, great tearing sobs that pulsed out of her like blood out of a wound.

"That was a low thing to say." He ground out his words. "I'm sorry. Corrie, I'm sorry, I'm sorry..." He bent, his face contorting with self-contempt, and his mouth traveled over her wan face in soft, tender kisses that sipped away the tears and the pain and the hurt, finally ending against the soft trembling of her mouth. "Corrie," he groaned as he nibbled at her lips.

She put her hand up to his face and pressed it hard against his mouth. "Don't," she pleaded.

The hand was trembling. He warmed it in his own and brought it hungrily to his mouth, palm up.

"How could you take such a risk?" he demanded huskily, lifting his mouth from her hand. She tried to pull it away, but he didn't let go of it even then, and his face was hard, like the glittery eyes that watched her without even blinking.

"You don't care if I die," she accused shakenly.

He winced. "Do you think I want you dead?" he asked roughly.

Her eyes were sad and bitter. "Don't you?" she asked on a harsh laugh. "Would you forgive me for Barry's death if I died, too?"

He drew in a harsh breath. It had become painfully clear to him that he could hurt her badly.

There was a soft knock on the door and Sandy walked in, raising her eyebrows at the sight of Ted standing by Coreen's bed, holding her hand.

"Did Ted tell you that you're coming home with me?" Sandy asked gently.

"That isn't necessary...!"

"Yes, it is," Ted said curtly. "We'll get a nurse for you."

Coreen panicked. "No!" she said. "No, I won't!"

"You will," he replied coldly. "If I have to pick you up and carry you in my arms every step of the way!"

Coreen felt the words in her heart. She averted her eyes. He hadn't meant it personally, of course. But the phrasing touched her deeply.

"You need to get some sleep," Sandy said gently. "I'll be back later."

"*We'll* be back later," Ted corrected, his eyes daring Coreen to argue with him. He glanced at Sandy. "She's on the fifth floor, and she might try to tie a few sheets together and parachute out of here."

Sandy laughed. Coreen's eyes were so tragic that it didn't last. "It's all right," she told her friend. "You'll be fine."

"Will I?" she asked, looking at Ted with open fear.

Sandy saw the way they were staring at each other, made an excuse and left them alone.

"What is it?" Ted asked softly.

She didn't reply. She simply shook her head, confusedly.

He stood beside her, watching her eyes. "It was only a kiss," he said quietly. "I know I shouldn't have done it, but you frightened me."

She searched his lean face. "Frightened you?"

He pushed his hands deep into his pockets to keep from reaching for her. His emotions were teetering on a knife-edge. "We thought you were dying until we got here."

"I'm not suicidal," she said firmly, "regardless of what you think. I love skydiving. I only wanted to get away from the world for a little while."

"You almost got away permanently. Skydiving in a thunderstorm!"

"It wasn't raining when I went up. Haven't you ever done anything the least bit dangerous?" she asked.

"Why, yes," he replied, holding her eyes. "I kissed you," he said dryly, and walked out of the room before she could respond.

* * *

Ted lifted a rigid Coreen out of the wheelchair and carried her to the car, while Sandy held the door open. Coreen thanked the nurses and hesitantly linked her arms around Ted's neck.

"I'm heavy," she protested when he picked her up.

His face was very close to hers, so close that his eyes filled the world. "You hardly weigh anything at all," he said bitterly.

She grimaced. "That isn't what that tiny intern said when he had to heft me onto the cart."

He laughed. It was a sound that Coreen had never heard before, and her expression said so.

Her eyes were drowning him in warm, unfamiliar feelings. He shifted her a little roughly as he turned and started toward the car, still holding her eyes. "Is this how you got your claws into Barry?" he asked under his breath. "Looking at him with those soft, hungry eyes?"

She averted her face and stiffened even more in his arms. "Think what you like about me, Ted. I don't care."

"Yes, you do," he said through his teeth. "That's what makes it so damned unforgivable."

"What?"

He glared down at her. "You were married and you still lusted after me," he said harshly. "You denied your husband because of it, and he knew it. It was why he drank. It was why he died," he added, growing colder inside as the guilt ate at him. "He told me, didn't you know? Do you think I could ever forgive you for that?"

The bitterness in him was damning. She couldn't deny it now because they were within Sandy's earshot. It wouldn't have mattered regardless, because he had his own opinion and he wouldn't change it. She hadn't used him to hurt Barry, it was the other way around. But he liked his opinion of her. It reinforced his warped view of women.

He put her in the back seat, so that she could stretch out, and she didn't say another word. She left all the conversation to him and Sandy. There wasn't much.

The bedroom they gave her was done in soft beiges and pinks, and the bed was a huge four-poster.

"The bed was Ted's once," Sandy said when she'd tucked her friend up, "but he wanted something less antiquated when we redecorated the house."

Coreen tingled all over, thinking that Ted had once slept where she was lying. It would probably be the closest she ever got to him, she thought on a silent laugh. Now he had even more reason to blame her for Barry's death. He would feel guilty that Barry was denied a happy marriage because his wife didn't want him, she wanted Ted.

"I'll go see about something for us to eat. We drove up without lunch. Are you hungry?"

"I had a little gelatin and some soup," Corrie recalled. "It was nice, but I could eat a sandwich."

"No sooner said than done."

She left and Coreen shifted the pillows behind her. She was wearing a sleeveless white cotton gown with a high neckline and a tiny blue and pink embroidered flower pattern in the bodice that drew no attention at all to her small, high breasts. She wished she had a robe, but she'd forgotten to ask Sandy to stop by the house and get one. It didn't matter. She was covered the way a Victorian spinster might be. She grimaced when she remembered the low-cut fashions she'd worn only two years before, things she could never wear again. Not now.

The door opened and Ted walked in. He'd changed into jeans and boots and an open-necked chambray shirt, and he looked rangy and dangerous.

Her eyes fell to the opening at his throat where thick hair peeked out. She'd never seen Ted without a shirt. She'd never seen Ted much at all, except in the distance.

If she was looking, so was he. His eyes had found the embroidery and he was staring at it with interest.

She jerked the sheet up to her collarbone irritably. "They're just marbles," she said without thinking.

He smiled. It was unconscious and instinctive, because she looked so angry, lying there with her poor bruised face. "Not quite," he mused.

She glared at him. "Sandy's fixing something to eat."

"I know. When she's through destroying the kitchen, I'll cook a few omelets."

"She said she was making sandwiches. Anyone can make a sandwich."

"Not without bread, and Mrs. Bird told me at breakfast that she'd made toast with the last of it. Sandy's trying to cook steaks."

"Oh, dear," she said, because she'd been threatened with Sandy's steaks several times in the past.

Ted's head lifted. He heard the muttered curses coming from the kitchen and smelled smoke. "There goes the first one."

"You might stop her," she suggested.

"Not with all those knives in there," he replied. He moved closer to the bed and sat down beside her. He held her eyes and suddenly pulled the sheet away, staying it when she tried to make a grab for it.

"Let go of it, Ted," she warned.

"What are you afraid of?" he asked with a quizzical smile. "Sandy's within shouting range."

"What are you doing?" she returned uneasily.

His lean hand pressed palm-down over her breastbone, shocking her into stillness. His hand was so big that his fingers spread halfway over one small breast. He let it rest there, waiting for her to react.

Coreen grabbed his wrist, trying to remove his hand. She was sore there, and she didn't want him to feel the stitches. She tugged hard and then lay there gaping at him, with eyes so big they looked like blue china saucers.

He might have found that reaction very strange in a woman who'd been married for almost two years, if he hadn't known she was frigid. Her resistance to his touch after the funeral and now was beginning to eat at his curiosity. If Barry had told the truth, and Coreen had harbored a dark passion for Ted, then why was she avoiding his touch so arduously? It disturbed him somehow to know that she didn't hunger for his kisses anymore. Her actions had implications that he wasn't certain he was ready to face just yet. She hadn't been frigid two years ago....

He scowled as he finally let her lift his hand away and push it aside.

"What did you think you were doing?" she asked, flustered.

"Experimenting," he said. "For a woman who's panting lustfully after me, you're surprisingly reluctant to be touched."

"I'm not...lusting after you." She choked, averting her eyes.

"So I noticed. Then why did you hold me over Barry's head?" he asked with faint distaste.

It wasn't easy to appear calm when she was churning inside. "I didn't," she said wearily.

"No?" One lean hand was resting beside her body. He looked down at her breasts and she tugged the sheet over them. He lifted an eyebrow. "Overreacting a bit, aren't you? I haven't touched you there."

"I'm not an art exhibit," she informed him. "And you needn't say that you wouldn't buy any tickets, because I know it already! You told me why over two years ago."

His pale eyes slid over her face and up to meet her angry gaze. "In the most cruel way I could find," he agreed, and there was a hint of regret in his voice. "Did Sandy ever tell you why?"

"Yes," she said. "But I never hurt you."

"No, although you were pretty persistent for a while there." His eyes searched hers quietly. "I wanted you out of my hair."

"Congratulations. You succeeded."

His jaw tautened. "Why did you marry Barry?"

The question came like a lightning bolt. She started from the sudden shock of it. She couldn't bear to tell him the truth. She averted her eyes. "He asked me."

"And you accepted, just like that?" he asked impatiently.

"He looked after Dad when no one else bothered," she said simply. "We were down to our last dollar. He not only bought the feed store, but he also advanced us the cash to keep Dad's doctor bills paid while the paperwork was finalized. I owed him so much. Marriage seemed a very small price to pay for my father's peace of mind," she finished, without telling him the whole truth of it, that his own attitude had pushed her right into Barry's arms. If Ted had been just a little more sympathetic... but it didn't bear thinking about.

He got up from the bed abruptly and strode to the window. He rested one shoulder against the windowsill and stared out at the lush green pastures where black-coated cattle were grazing; his prize black Angus.

"Did you love him?" he asked.

She twisted the pretty edging of the sheet. "I was... fond of him, at first."

He looked at her. "Did you ever want him, even at the beginning?"

She shuddered. She wasn't quick enough to hide it.

"You wanted me," he said coldly. "I haven't forgotten the party at the gun club, even if you have. You would have given me anything that night."

"You wouldn't have taken it," she said somberly, staring at him unblinking. "You even told me why. Remember?"

He averted his gaze back to the pasture. He didn't like remembering the things he'd said to her. Absently he pulled a cigarette out of his pocket. But he only looked at it for a minute and pushed it back into the pack with a wry smile in her direction.

"I promised Sandy I'd quit," he explained.

"Imagine you doing something a mere woman wanted," she murmured.

"Sandy's my sister."

"And the only woman you like."

He turned, leaning his back against the sill. He folded his arms and crossed his long legs, surveying her with pursed lips and an odd little smile. "I could like you, if I tried," he said. He jerked away from the window. "But I'm not going to try."

"Of course not," she agreed. "What would be the point?"

He paused beside the bed. "You aren't going to be able to do much for a few weeks, in your condition," he said. "I hope you like it here, because you're staying for the duration, even if I have to tie you up."

She sat up in bed, grimacing at the pain, her blue eyes angry. "I could go home . . ."

"You don't have a home anymore," he said bluntly.

She lay back down, wincing at the pain. She felt broken and bruised. Her eyes closed, to shut him out. "No. I haven't, have I?" she agreed.

He hated her lack of spirit. His pale eyes lanced over her dark hair and narrowed as he saw the silver threads that meandered through it. "Why, you're going gray, Coreen," he said, surprised.

"Yes." Her eyes opened. "Your hair used to be the color of mine, didn't it?" she asked.

"Not since I turned thirty. It grayed prematurely. It's even gone gray on my chest."

"Has it? I didn't notice."

He lifted an eyebrow, because her gaze had seemed to be locked to his throat when he'd first entered the room.

"Damn, damn, damn!" echoed down the hall from the kitchen, along with a more pungent smell of smoke.

"I'd better get in there while there's some beef left in the freezer. I'll send her to keep you company while I cook."

"I can cook," she said hesitantly. "I used to do all the cooking at home, before I married."

He lifted an eyebrow. "Did you?" he asked indifferently. "I never noticed."

She averted her eyes. He couldn't have made it more plain than that, but she'd known that he never paid attention to her while Barry was courting her. She watched him leave the room with sad, resigned eyes, mourning the woman she'd been. He hadn't wanted her when she was whole. There was no chance that he'd want her now, in her damaged condition. And even if he did, she reminded herself, she had nothing left to give him.

Chapter Four

Coreen had only the one gown to wear, and none of her clothes. She wanted to remind them that she needed her things from the house she'd shared with Barry, but she was apprehensive about letting anyone go there to see the room she'd occupied. Fortunately, Ted's housekeeper, Mrs. Bird, had a daughter about Coreen's size who'd married and gone to live overseas. Mrs. Bird brought her an armload of pretty things on loan, and she told Sandy that she didn't need anything else at the moment. Things were hectic for the first few days she was in residence, anyway. Sandy had to go to work and Ted had two mares in foal. He stayed out with his horses most of the time, while a grateful Coreen was left pretty much to herself in the daytime. She didn't mind. Having Ted near her was disconcerting and made her nervous.

She sat at the window in her room every day and watched him work the horses out in the corral. He was gentle with his horses, patient and kind. Coreen wished that she'd had such kindness from him.

There was a particular horse that she favored, a thoroughbred, which was coal black with a white blaze on his forehead and white stockings on all four feet. There had been a similar horse that Sandy always loaned her when they went riding. Not that this one could be the same horse. It was much younger than the horse Sandy had let her borrow. It might be a descendant, though.

She knew that she shouldn't be spying on Ted, but it gave her such pleasure to look at him. He was long and lean and he moved with the liquid grace of a cowboy. He could spin a lariat so expertly that no horse ever escaped his noose. He could ride bareback as easily as he could ride in a saddle. His temper was quick and hot, and she'd seen him lose it once with one of his men over some equipment. She'd moved away from the open window, shivering with reaction. Barry had always yelled when he was going to hit her. It was probably just as well that Ted didn't want any part of her, she assured herself, because she was as intimidated by his temper as she was by his strength.

All the same, she couldn't keep away from the window. Her mind rolled back the terrible time in between, and she was a young woman again, in love with Ted and full of hope that he might care one day.

It was inevitable that Ted would notice her blatant interest. The silent figure by the window was drawing attention, and not only from the recipient. Ted's men had begun to rag him gently about Coreen's "calf eyes" following him around wherever he went.

Ted came by her room late on the day before Sandy was due back and paused in the doorway. "Do you want a tray in your room tonight, as usual?" he asked curtly.

She was surprised by his hostility as much as by the question. She'd had her meals on trays ever since her arrival, which was perfectly fine with her; she couldn't eat with Ted glaring across a table at her. She fumbled around for a reply.

"Sandy won't be back until tomorrow," he reminded her. "And I have a date tonight. She's an attorney from Victoria who's having supper here."

She could tell that he'd hoped to shock her. He had. She couldn't hide her reaction quickly enough to escape his pointed scrutiny. "I...wouldn't want to intrude. A tray in my room is fine," she said quickly.

He stared at her with one narrowed eye, his face cold and hard. "You need something to do with your time while you're here."

She didn't know how to take this frontal assault. She just stared at him.

"Something besides watching me out the window every time I move," he added bluntly.

She averted her face with a caught breath. "I was watching the horses, not you," she said.

"All the same, you'll be happier with something to occupy you." He didn't add that so would he, but then, he didn't have to.

Her hands, unseen, clenched on her robe. He was putting the knife in already. She'd thought that her condition might win her just enough sympathy to keep his hostility at bay. She was wrong.

"Yes," she agreed without looking up. "I would . . . like something to do."

He studied her down-bent head with mingled feelings, the strongest of which was guilt. She'd driven her husband to drink and ultimately caused him to die, all because she wanted a man she couldn't have and taunted her husband with him. Ted had felt the guilt like a knife in his gut ever since he'd heard about Barry's death. Coreen's presence was aggravating his self-contempt. She was a constant reminder of the pain his cousin had suffered.

He'd deliberately invited Lillian over for supper, not because he really wanted to, but because it was important to make Coreen understand that he still wasn't interested in her. He couldn't bear having his unwanted houseguest stare at him longingly through the curtains. He couldn't even avoid her while he worked, for God's sake!

"This isn't going to work out," he said aloud, his eyes narrow and cold.

"You might not believe it, but I tried to tell Sandy that," she said with a faint smile. She lifted her eyes. "I'll start looking for a place the minute I can stand up without falling."

He shifted restlessly. "I'll see if I can help you."

"Thank you," she said with the dregs of her dignity. It had taken quite a bruising already. "And nothing expensive, please. I still have to find a job."

"There may be some way to break provisions in Barry's will," he said curtly. "I'll check into it. Failing that,

I'll make sure that you have a living allowance, at least.''

She started to express her thanks again, but she felt like a parrot. She just nodded.

"I'll send Mrs. Bird along to see what you want to eat.''

"Whatever she's cooking will be fine,'' she replied with stilted courtesy. "I wouldn't want to cause any more trouble than I already have.''

He didn't answer her. His eyes were still cold, accusing, when he turned and went down the hall. It wasn't until he reached his own room that he remembered the devastation Coreen had faced in one week. Whether or not she loved Barry, she'd been widowed, injured, and she'd lost her home and her income. A man would have to be made of stone to feel no pity at all for such a victim of circumstances. He blamed her for too much, perhaps. She looked very fragile in that big, four-poster bed, and he didn't like the way he felt after being so savage to her.

But he put his guilt aside with his working clothes. He showered and changed into a neat pair of white slacks with a stripped designer shirt, a linen sport coat and tie. Then, without seeing Coreen again, he drove to the Jacobsville airport to meet Lillian's flight from Victoria.

Coreen was getting more and more depressed. She could hear Ted and his houseguest all the way down the hall, laughing and talking, as if they were old and good friends. Probably they were.

She didn't know how she could bear much more of Ted's reluctant hospitality. If Sandy had been here, it would have been different. She couldn't expect her best friend to give up her job just to keep Coreen company. Sandy had to travel, which meant that Coreen would be stuck here often with just Ted and Mrs. Bird for company.

Mrs. Bird had brought her a tray, grumbling about their dinner guest.

"Wants her coffee weaker and her salad with dressing on the side," Mrs. Bird harrumphed, swinging her ample figure around as she placed the tray over Coreen's lap. "Doesn't care for beef, because it has cholesterol, and dessert is out of the question."

"She must be healthy," Coreen remarked as she savored the smell of the cheese soup and freshly baked bread she'd been served.

"Skinny as a rail. They say it's going to be the new fad." She eyed Coreen critically, seeing the hollows in her cheeks. "Nothing like cheese soup and bread to fatten up little skeletons."

"I haven't had much appetite. But this is wonderful," she said with honest enjoyment, and smiled.

The housekeeper smiled back. "I made apple pie for dessert with apples I dried myself."

Coreen was impressed. "I love apple pie!"

"So I was told, and with ice cream. You'll get that, too." She grinned at Coreen and went back toward the door. "Just set that by the bed and I'll get it later, after they've gone. On their way to a play at the civic center, they said, then he has to take her back to the airport to catch a late flight."

"Is she nice?" Coreen asked curiously.

The older woman hesitated, her gray hair stringy from long hours in the kitchen.

"Well, I suppose she is, in her own way. She's stylish and real smart, and she and Ted have known each other for a long time. Expected them to get married once, she was that crazy about him. But Ted doesn't want to get married. Broke her heart. They're friends still, but don't you think she wouldn't jump at the chance to marry him."

"I guess he can be nice when he likes," Coreen said without committing herself. She started eating her soup.

"Nice to some," Mrs. Bird said, faintly puzzled. "Well, I'll leave you to it."

"Thank you."

"No trouble. It's a pleasure to see people enjoy their food."

Coreen finished her lonely meal and put the tray aside. She wished she had something to read, but there wasn't even a magazine, much less television or a radio. She felt cut off from the world in the pretty antique bedroom.

The laughter from the other room grated on her nerves. She tried to imagine Ted laughing with her, wanting her company, enjoying conversation like that. He only ever seemed to scowl when he was with her. Lillian must be special to him. She didn't want to be jealous. She had no right. He laughed again, and Coreen felt the hot sting of tears.

Her blurred vision cleared on the face of the clock. It was only seven o'clock. She hoped that she could go to sleep, to block out the sound of Ted's pleasure in the other woman. She turned off her light and closed her eyes with bitter resignation. Incredibly she slept the night through.

* * *

The next day, she didn't watch out the window while Ted worked his horses. She put on a pair of too-large jeans and an equally large T-shirt with a Texas logo on it and curled up in a chair to read the paper she'd begged from Mrs. Bird.

The news was depressing. She glanced at the comics page, and finally settled on the word puzzle. It kept her mind busy, so that she wouldn't remember that Ted wanted her out of his house. She was still too wobbly and sore to do much. An employer was going to expect more than she was capable of giving just yet. She hoped Sandy would come home today. Her friend would help her escape from this prison Ted had made for her. He hadn't told her to stay in her room, but he'd made it very obvious that he didn't want her around him.

It was after lunch when she heard a car drive up. Minutes later, a smiling Sandy came into the room and fell onto the bed in an exaggerated pose.

"I'm tired!" she groaned, smiling at Coreen. "I thought I'd never get that new computer system put together for our client. But I did. Now I can take a day off and spend some time with you. How's it been going?"

"Just fine," Coreen said blithely. "Could you help me find an apartment?"

Sandy's expression was comical. "I gather that Ted's been at it again?" she muttered.

"We've had this discussion before," Coreen said quietly. "You know how he feels about me, about having me here. He's accused me of leering at him again, and maybe I have. God help me, I can't seem to stop..." She bit her lip. "Only, it isn't leering and it isn't lust. You can't know how it was with Barry," she added, her eyes wide and tragic. "If you did, you'd realize how incredible it is that I can even look at a man without shuddering!"

Sandy sat up, brushing her hair out of her eyes. "Maybe if you talked to Ted..."

"Why?" Coreen asked solemnly. "He doesn't want to know anything about my marriage, or about me. He's made it very clear that I'm here on sufferance and that he isn't interested in me."

"Mrs. Bird mentioned that Lillian came to supper last night," the other woman murmured. "Did you get to meet her?"

Coreen shook her head.

Sandy sighed angrily. "He can't help the way he is. I'm sorry, Corrie. I'm very sorry that I finagled you into this corner. I had hoped...well, that's not important now. Do you want out?"

"Yes, please" came the immediate reply.

"Okay. We can both move up to Victoria, into my old apartment. I never have gotten around to leasing it, so it's still empty. It's plenty big enough for both of us, and you won't have my brother to contend with."

"But your job..."

"I work at our branch office in Victoria as well as the headquarter office in Houston," Sandy reminded her.

"I don't want to impose," Coreen said firmly.

"You're my best friend. How could you impose?"

"I'll need my things from the house," she said hesitantly. "I hate to ask, but could you...?"

"Of course I can go get them for you."

"Henry has a key. He's still living in the chauffeur's quarters, I'm sure, because Tina will need him to take care of the place until she moves in. My clothes will be in the closet, in the second bedroom on the right up-stairs. There isn't much in the drawers, and I'd already packed up my own books and tapes, and the few things mother gave me."

"I'll run down there this afternoon, if you like."

"Thank you, Sandy."

"What are friends for? Now you stop worrying! By next week, we'll be in Victoria and all these bad memories will be just that."

Sandy went to get them some coffee and cake, which they ate with relish. Ted came in just after Sandy had gone to change her clothes and get some suitcases to pack Coreen's dresses in.

Coreen was still sitting in the armchair by the win-dow. She flushed when he looked at her. "I was talking to Sandy, not leering at you out the window," she said with faint defensiveness.

His pale eyes narrowed. "It's a hell of a pity you didn't spend some of that misplaced longing on poor Barry," he said mockingly.

Her features grew very still. "He had women," she said.

"No wonder, if he had a wife who wouldn't let him touch her," he returned. His face held such distaste that she squirmed in her chair. "You tormented him and then you let him get in a car when he'd been drinking," he said curtly. "I won't ever forget, or forgive, that. You ended up with nothing and that's all you deserved. My God, the very sight of you sickens me!" he added roughly, and the contempt in his eyes hurt her for an instant before he turned away and continued on down the hall.

She didn't move until he was out of sight. The pain went even too deep for tears. She thought of how it was going to be for another week, before she and Sandy left for Victoria, knowing exactly how Ted felt about her, what he thought, and having to face his scorn day after endless day. She couldn't take it. She couldn't take any more. She was going to have to get away now.

If she waited until Sandy left to pick up her clothes, Ted would probably leave shortly thereafter. Then she could get a cab to the depot and a bus to Houston. She had just enough money for a flight. There was surely a YWCA in Houston, where she could stay. Even that would be infinitely better than here, with Ted tormenting her in reprisal for his cousin's death. If she'd been stronger, she'd have fought him tooth and nail. But she hadn't the heart for any more fighting right now. She only hoped she had enough strength to get out of here.

Sandy, unaware of Ted's visit, popped her head in the door. "I'm going. Ted said that he'll drive me over to your house. I'll be back in a couple of hours. Bye!"

Coreen had wanted to catch her eye and tell her she was leaving, but Sandy was already on her way out the front door. She heard her call something to Mrs. Bird. Two car doors slammed and an engine revved up.

Thirty harrowing minutes later, she said a hesitant goodbye to Mrs. Bird, asking first if she could have the loan of the clothes she was wearing, with a pair of Sandy's shoes, just until she could get her own.

"But I thought Sandy and Ted were going over to the house to get your things," Mrs. Bird said, puzzled.

"I'm meeting them there," Coreen lied glibly. "I just remembered some things I need that they won't know about."

"But, dear, you're just not in any shape to be trying to do something like this!"

"I'm doing just fine," Coreen assured her with a gentle smile. "Thank you so much for your kindness. I won't ever forget you."

Mrs. Bird was frowning now. "You should wait. Let me call over at your house and make sure they're there."

"It won't matter, honestly, I'll be fine." She heard the horn and smiled her relief. "There's the taxi I called. Now don't worry, all right?"

Mrs. Bird grimaced. "You're so pale."

"I'm a trooper. I'll be fine." She clutched her purse closer. It was all she had left of her own right now, all her worldly possessions. "I'll be in touch."

"You're coming back, aren't you?"

"I may stay at the house," she lied. "I'll see what they think," she added deliberately. "Okay?"

Mrs. Bird relaxed. "Okay. Be careful, now."

"Oh, I will. I will. Goodbye."

Coreen made her way outside very slowly, grimacing as her bruised ribs protested the movement. She was weak and not as steady on her feet as she would have liked, but she made it to the cab with as much haste as possible. Her heart was going like a jackhammer and she was tense with nerves. She couldn't bear the thought that she might be stopped at the last minute. She got in, waving at Mrs. Bird, and gave him her destination. As she rode away, she sighed with relief. She was free at last. There would be no more torment. Barry was gone and soon she'd be away from Ted. Then maybe she could have some peace again.

Ted and Sandy had found Henry, the chauffeur, in his small apartment when they got to the house to get

Coreen's things. Henry had the keys. He unlocked the front door and showed them up to her room, his whole mood somber.

"Poor kid," he said as they opened her closet and stopped dead at the sight that met their eyes. "He kept her poor for two years, hounded her and harassed her, brought her back every time she tried to run away. I hated working for him, but I couldn't leave her here to cope with it by herself."

Ted's eyes flashed dangerously as he turned from his shocked contemplation of the three dresses in the huge closet to stare angrily at the older man.

"My cousin had millions of dollars," he began.

Henry nodded. "Yes, sir, he did, and he bought himself the best clothes and the best cars and the best women in Houston," he added, not backing down an inch from the threatening set of Ted's lithe body. "But all Coreen got was the back of his hand and the edge of his tongue. He cut her bad that last night he slept here, the night before the party. I had to drive her to the doctor and lie about how she got that way, with him barely sober and standing right there beside her and swearing she fell on a sheet of tin. I never saw so much blood..."

Ted and Sandy had both gone very still.

"He cut her? With what?" Ted demanded, his expression one of angry disbelief.

"With a knife, Mr. Regan," Henry said. "He had her down in the living room on the couch when I came in to see if he needed anything before I went to bed. He was cursing her, and threatening to kill her. I thought I'd talked some sense into him, but he kept cursing her about some birthday card she'd got and accused her of being unfaithful," he added, frowning curiously at the expression that washed over Ted's face. "He cut her before I could get to him. She screamed and the blood went everywhere. That seemed to bring him to his senses. We took her to the doctor and got her sewed up, then he went back out again. We didn't see him all of the next day—not until he came home to take her to that party with him.''

Ted sat down in a chair. ''It was over a birthday card?''

''Yes, sir. Seemed to make him crazy. He used to hit her sometimes. She never talked about it, but I could see the bruises. I'm glad he's dead,'' he added icily. ''He was a brute, and I don't care if he was your cousin, he got what he deserved. He was going to bring her back here that night and start on her again. He'd probably have killed her, but I wouldn't let her leave the party with him. He'd already dismissed me when he dragged her out front, and he was threatening her again. Nobody heard but the three of us. The gossip was just that she let him drive drunk.'' Henry's dark eyes narrowed. ''She didn't do anything except save herself from being cut worse than she already had been, or maybe killed. In the mood he was in, drinking like he was, he could have done anything to her.''

''You're lying,'' Ted said through his teeth. His face had gone pasty.

He turned to Sandy, aware that Ted wasn't being responsive. ''You get her to show you the stitches, Miss Regan,'' Henry returned, talking to her. ''It was a bad cut. The doctor thinks she's just clumsy, because of all those things that happened to her. Mr. Barry is what happened to her,'' he added. ''She never crashed in any glider... he knocked her down a flight of stairs!''

Ted's indrawn breath was audible. He put his head in his hands and Sandy ushered Henry out of the room, thanking him for his help. Ted hadn't moved when she got back and closed the door.

She didn't say a word. He looked as if his conscience was killing him already.

"Did you know?" he asked finally, raising a tortured face to hers.

"No," she replied heavily. "I believed what she told me, just as you did. Barry wouldn't let me see her at all. We had to meet for lunch secretly, and she never talked about her marriage. Nobody knew. Except Henry, apparently."

Ted got to his feet. "She can't know what we've found out," he said slowly.

"Of course not."

He glanced at her. "There's more than this, I imagine," he said with the beginning of horror in his eyes.

She only nodded.

He turned, his heart stilled in his chest as he remembered what he'd said to Coreen just before he and Sandy had come over here. He probably couldn't undo the damage he'd done. He'd spent too much time hurting Coreen.

Sandy was staring at him and he hadn't been aware of her question. "What?" he murmured absently.

"I said, what are we going to do about Corrie?"

"For now," he said with a heavy sigh, "let's just get her stuff packed and get out of here."

Chapter Five

Ted carried the bags into the house. Only one of them had been needed to hold Coreen's pitiful few things. The others they'd carried were empty. It was only just beginning to sink in that Coreen had been the victim, not his cousin. Barry had lied to him from the very beginning, and because of those lies, he'd been cruel to Coreen. It was unbearable to remember it. Poor little thing, broken and bruised and terrified, and all she'd had from him was more humiliation and blame. He'd given her nothing else, in all the time he'd known her.

Mrs. Bird had gone home by the time they'd arrived. She left supper in the kitchen and a note saying that Coreen had promised to be in touch.

Ted read it twice, but it still hadn't quite made sense when a tight-lipped Sandy came back into the kitchen. "Her room is empty," she said. "She's gone."

"Gone?" He exploded. "My God, she could barely walk! Where could she have gone?"

"I have no idea," Sandy said miserably, dropping into a chair. "She doesn't have a relative in the world. And it's a big world, too. She has the borrowed clothes on her back and she has less than a hundred dollars in her purse. Her credit cards won't do her any good. I'm sure Tina has canceled them all by now."

Ted muttered under his breath, ramming his hands deep into his pockets. "Any guesses?"

"I'll phone Mrs. Bird. She might have said something before she left. Failing that, I'll start telephoning cab companies. What I can't understand is why she left so suddenly," she said, shaking her head as she picked up the telephone receiver and began to press numbered buttons. "I'd already promised her that we'd move up to my apartment in Victoria next week."

"When did you talk about that?" he demanded suddenly.

"Just before you came in... Hello, Mrs. Bird? Yes, do you know where Coreen went? You don't? Then do you know what cab company... yes, I know the one. Thanks. No, it's all right, we'll find her, don't worry."

She hung up and started thumbing through the telephone directory, while Ted stared at the floor and cursed himself.

He knew there would be no hope of finding her before dark. He only hoped she had enough money to stay at a decent hotel, with doors that would lock. He refused to let Sandy go with him while he searched. It was his fault that she'd run away. Now he had to persuade her to come back. It wasn't going to be easy.

Coreen was sitting quietly in the common room of the YWCA when he arrived. She looked tired and sick, and a woman who looked as if she might be a social worker was sitting with her, taking notes on a clipboard.

Ted felt his whole body tensing when he got close enough to hear what was being said.

"...unlikely that we can place you until you're in better physical condition, Mrs. Tarleton, but in the meanwhile we can work on finding accommodation for you. Now..."

"She has accommodation already," Ted said quietly.

Coreen's head turned and her eyes mirrored her horror. She went deathly pale and gripped the arms of the chair for dear life as Ted came closer, tall and elegant in his gray suit and matching Stetson and boots. The only splash of color was in the conservative stripe of his white shirt and the paisley tie he wore with it. He looked very rich.

"Do you know this man, Coreen?" the social worker asked suspiciously.

"He's my best friend's brother," Coreen managed to say. "And he needn't have come here. I can take care of myself."

"She has a cracked rib and some deep lacerations from a skydiving accident," Ted told the older woman quietly. "She's been staying with us while she got better. There's been a misunderstanding."

The older woman's eyes narrowed. "Considering the condition Mrs. Tarleton arrived here in, I should think that is an understatement Mr....?"

"Regan," he said shortly. "Ted Regan."

It was a name that was known in south Texas. The woman's arrogance retreated. "I see."

"No, you don't. But we'll see that Coreen is properly cared for. She was recently widowed."

"A misfortune," the woman said. And before Ted could agree, her eyes hardened and she added, "Because after speaking with another social worker in Jacobsville this morning, I should have enjoyed bringing her late husband before a grand jury."

Ted didn't respond as Coreen had expected him to, in ready defense of his cousin. He didn't reply at all. She had protested that telephone call, but the social worker had been adamant about getting to the truth. In the end, Coreen was too shell-shocked to refuse her answers.

"Where are your things, Coreen?" he asked, and his tone wasn't one she recognized.

Her frantic eyes met those of the social worker. "I don't have to go, do I?" she asked in a hoarse whisper.

Ted's face contorted before he got it under control. His hand went deep into his pocket and clenched there. "It's all right," he said, controlling the urge to pick her up and run for it. "I'm going to be away on business. Sandy will be all alone at the house. She'd enjoy having you keep her company."

She had so few options. She was tired and hurting more than ever from her physical wounds with all the exertion she'd been forced to make. The emotional wounds were even worse. She looked up at Ted with a tortured expression.

"You'll never have cause to run away again, Coreen," he said huskily, his features rigid. "I swear you won't!"

She didn't trust him. It was in her eyes. She averted them to the social worker, and saw the indecision there. The woman would fight for her if she could. But Ted Regan was powerful, much more formidable than Barry had ever been.

It was the past all over again. Money and power, taking charge, taking control, taking over. She couldn't run. She had no energy left.

"I'll go back," she said in a defeated tone.

"Your things?"

She gestured at the small, thin bag. "This is all I have."

His expression fascinated the social worker, who thought she'd seen them all.

"You will take care of her?" the older woman asked with a last, faint worry.

He nodded. He didn't trust his voice to speak. Coreen stood up, but when he offered his hand, she moved out of reach. Her eyes didn't quite make it to his face as she turned to thank the social worker before she moved toward the door.

His car, a sleek Jaguar, was sitting right outside the door. He helped her into the passenger seat and went around to get in beside her, stowing his Stetson upside-down on the hat carrier above the visor.

Coreen's hands clenched over the legs of her loose, borrowed jeans. She stared at them, noticing idly that her small, thin wedding band was still on her ring finger. Barry had given her that one piece of jewelry; no other. She didn't know why she was still wearing it, after all this time.

Ted noticed her tension. "I'm sorry," he said curtly.

She looked out the windshield, unmoving, unmoved. "Sandy shouldn't have made you come."

"Sandy doesn't make me do anything," he said quietly. "I apologize for the things I said to you, Coreen."

She didn't understand his change of heart, and she didn't trust it. She didn't answer.

He knew that it was going to be difficult. He hadn't realized that all his apologies were going to be futile as well. She wouldn't even look at him.

He started the car and drove them quickly and efficiently back to Jacobsville.

Mrs. Bird had lunch ready by the time they arrived, but Coreen was too worn-out to eat any. Refusing Ted's help, she let Sandy ease her down the hall and back into bed again. Mrs. Bird came in right behind her, fussing and coaxing until she got her to eat a sandwich. But she'd barely swallowed it down when the long, uncertain hours caught up with her. She closed her eyes and went to sleep.

Ted looked up as Sandy joined him in the living room. "How is she?" he asked.

"Sleeping. Poor little thing, she's worn-out. Why did she do it?" she added. "Did she tell you?"

With a set expression, he moved to his desk and picked up the telephone. "I'm going to fly up to Kansas and check on a stallion I'm thinking of buying."

Sandy was beginning to get a picture she didn't like. "You said something to her, didn't you?" she began.

"It's ancient history now," he replied. "She's safe from me. I won't hurt her anymore."

"So you think she's finally paid enough for the privilege of loving you? How kind of you," Sandy returned angrily.

His fingers trembled a little on the telephone face. "She doesn't love me," he replied coolly. "She was infatuated. That's all it was."

"You're sure?"

"If she'd loved me, she wouldn't have married my cousin, much less have stayed with him for two years," he said.

"As I remember, you were singularly unkind to her while her father was dying, Ted," Sandy reminded him as she got up from the sofa. "Barry pretended to be kind and gentle and offered her comfort, something you never did."

His face contorted as he stared sightlessly out the window. "Don't you think I know?" he growled.

She frowned, waiting. But he got the number he'd dialed, and business replaced torment in his deep voice.

Coreen didn't wake up until Ted had gone. Sandy sat with her for the rest of the day, and the one thing they didn't talk about in the hours that followed was Sandy's brother.

True to his word, Ted stayed away until he could put off his return no longer. Coreen got stronger by the day, and she was moving around with alacrity by the time Ted walked in the door one sunny afternoon.

She was laughing at something Sandy had said, her blue eyes full of humor, her elfin face smiling, aglow with pleasure. But she heard his step and turned her head, and all of it, every bit of it, went out of her like dying light. Ted felt suddenly empty. He'd dreamed over and over again of coming back and having Coreen's face light up when he walked in the door. It had once, years ago, for so brief a time. But it wasn't joy that claimed her features now. It was pain.

He couldn't bear to see it. He put his case down and greeted Sandy with what he thought was normal composure before he glanced at their houseguest.

"Hello, Coreen," he said with careful indifference.

"Ted." She didn't move, as if he had her in his sights and might fire at any minute. In the old jeans and ribbed knit top she was wearing, every thin line of her body was visible. Defensively, her arms folded over her breasts.

He forced his eyes away from her.

"Did you find your stallion before you went on to the cattleman's conference in Los Angeles?" Sandy asked pleasantly.

"Not really," he returned. He sat down and crossed his long legs. "I wasn't looking too hard."

"Lillian phoned twice while you were away," Sandy continued. "She said it was urgent."

"I'll call her later. How are you feeling, Coreen?"

"Much better, thanks," she replied. Her eyes sought his warily. "If you'd rather I left . . ."

"I wouldn't," he said curtly. His pale eyes sought hers and tried to hold them, but Coreen wasn't taking any more chances. She averted her own gaze to Sandy and smiled at her.

"Then I'll leave you two to talk," she said. She got to her feet, ignoring Ted's quiet protest that there was no need to absent herself. She walked out of the living room and back down the hall to the bedroom they'd given her.

"Well, what else did you expect?" Sandy asked when she heard the muffled curse leave his lips as he stood by the window. "She's had nothing but pain from men."

Ted reached for a cigarette and almost had it lit when Sandy took it from between his lips and tossed it into the fireplace.

"Stop that," she told him. "I'm tired of watching people try to kill themselves."

He glared at her. "You're not my keeper."

"You need one," she said shortly, her whole posture challenging. "Why don't you go and return Lillian's call? She's crazy about you, and old enough not to make you feel so guilty."

The innuendo didn't get past him. "Maybe I'll do that," he said, turning from the window. "Haven't you got something to do?"

"I had a date, but I broke it," she said. "I can't leave Coreen alone with you."

His eyes flashed dangerously in a face gone suddenly pale.

"Don't start rattling at me, you old snake," she returned. "I trust you, but she doesn't. I don't guess you've even noticed that she's afraid of you."

He stood very still. "What?"

"She's afraid of you, Ted," she repeated. "Good grief, don't you ever *look?*"

He let out a rough breath between his teeth and ran an angry hand around the back of his neck. "She never was before," he said defensively.

"That's right," she said. "Before she was married, she never once thought that a man would be physically cruel to her."

He rammed his hands into his pockets. "Damned little toad," he said huskily. "I pitied him, and there he was, feeding me lies about her to keep me angry, to keep me away so that I wouldn't know what he was doing to her!"

"Would you have cared?" Sandy challenged with a mocking laugh. "You're the last person on earth Coreen would look to for help!"

His broad chest rose and fell heavily as he struggled with memories that hurt him. "Then, or now?" he asked.

"What's the difference?" she replied. "You don't have to worry about her watching you anymore, by the way. She won't go near the window in her room, even to open it."

He made a sound under his breath and left the room, staring straight ahead with eyes that didn't even see.

Coreen had wandered outside on shaky legs to watch the horses. Ted was gone. She'd made sure before she'd ever left the house.

The jeans she was wearing were her own, the single pair she had. She wore sneakers and a loose top over it. It was overcast, with threatening weather, and she wondered if it would rain. The parched fields looked as if they could use some rain.

She paused at the stable door and frowned because she heard voices in the back, down the clean straw-aisle that ran widely from one open door to the other.

When Ted came out into the aisle, she turned quickly and started back toward the house.

"Coreen!"

His voice stopped her. She turned, her deep blue eyes wide and wary as they met his pale ones under the brim of his Stetson.

He was wearing working clothes, stained jeans with chaps and a patterned Western-cut shirt. His face was grim and he looked out of humor—as usual.

"I didn't know you were out here," she began defensively, coloring as he stared down at her.

"Oh, I know that," he said bitterly. "You leave rooms when I walk into them, you stay in your bedroom until I leave in the mornings, you won't even come out on the damned porch if you think I'm within a mile of my own house!"

Her lips parted on a shaky breath and she backed away from him.

"No...!" He bit down hard on his anger and took a deep breath. "Here, now, it's all right," he said, forcing himself to talk softly. "I'm not going to hurt you, Coreen," he added quizzically when her rigid posture showed no sign of relaxing.

She folded her arms over her breasts and just watched him, her whole stance wary, apprehensive.

He took off his Stetson and wiped his sweaty forehead on his sleeve. "Do you remember Amarillo, the horse Sandy used to let you borrow? He sired a foal by Merry Midnight. She's a two-year-old filly. We call her Topper. Want to see her?"

She softened toward him. She loved the horses. "Yes," she said after a minute.

He held out a hand. "Come on, then."

She moved toward him, but her arms stayed where they were.

He pretended not to notice that she wouldn't touch him. It was her feelings that mattered right now, not his own. He led her into the stable and out the back, to the back of the stable where the beautiful black horse with the white blaze and stockings stood in her big, clean stall grazing on fresh corn in a trough.

"Hello, Topper," he said to the horse. "Hello, girl."

He opened the corral door and motioned for Coreen to follow him. He smoothed his hand over the velvet nose and turned the horse's head so that Coreen could stroke her.

"Why, she's soft," she exclaimed.

"Like velvet, isn't she?" he mused, liking the way her eyes lit up with pleasure. He hadn't seen them that way in a long, long time.

"Why is she called Topper?"

He shrugged. "No particular reason. It seemed to fit. She's a two-year-old, and we hope she's going to make a thoroughbred racer. I've got a trainer coming soon to start working with her."

"A racer," she echoed. "You mean, like in the Kentucky Derby?"

"That's what we're hoping for next year," he confessed.

"Well, she's certainly beautiful enough," she had to admit.

He watched her stroke the horse's mane and ears. Topper paid her very little attention. She was intent on her breakfast.

A sudden clap of thunder made Topper jump. Coreen made a similar movement, gasping at the unexpected noise.

"Looks as if we may be in for a spring shower," he remarked, looking toward the sudden darkness outside the stable.

"Or a tornado," she added nervously.

"Oh, I don't think so," he said to reassure her. They moved out of the stall and he snapped the lock shut again before he strode to the back of the stable and looked out.

The sky was very dark, with blue-black clouds just over the horizon. Lightning flashed and a rumble of thunder followed it. "Beautiful, isn't it?" he remarked as he noticed her out of the corner of his eye. "Nature, in all her splendor."

"Violence," she corrected, shivering. Her eyes were apprehensive as she watched the lightning fork. "I hate loud noises."

He leaned against the wall and watched her curiously, his eyes intent on her wan face. "Loud noises, like a raised voice?" he asked gently.

She didn't look at him. "Something like that."

He moved away from the wall, and her eyes swept to encompass him, the same fear in them as the storm produced.

"Is it only loud noises, or is it men who come too close as well?" he queried.

She put up a defensive hand when he took another step toward her.

He saw her body tense. His pale eyes narrowed. Outside, the wind was growing bolder as the storm clouds darkened.

"Storms increase the number of negative ions in the atmosphere. Scientists say that we feel better when that happens," he remarked.

"Do they?" she murmured.

He drew in a slow, steady breath. "Coreen, I know about your marriage."

She laughed coldly. "Do you?"

"Harry told us. Everything."

The pseudosmile left her lips. She searched his eyes, looking for the truth. He hid his feelings very well. Nothing, nothing showed there.

"And you believed him?" she said after a shocked minute. "How amazing."

He grimaced. "Yes. I suppose that's how I thought you'd take it."

She averted her eyes to the storm and stiffened again when a violent thunderclap shook the ground. Rain was peppering down, splattering in the dust just outside the door. It would be impossible to get to the house now without getting wet. She couldn't run this time.

"Nothing's changed," she said. "Nothing at all."

He tossed his Stetson to one side and propped a boot on a bale of hay while they watched the rain come down. "We need that," he remarked. "We've just started planting hay."

"Have you?"

He started to reach for a cigarette to calm his nerves when he realized that Sandy had taken his last pack out of his shirt pocket. He laughed softly.

Coreen glanced at him.

"Sandy's stolen my smokes," he explained lazily. "She thinks cigarettes will kill me. She can't talk me into stopping, so she's gone militant."

"Oh."

He raised an eyebrow and smiled amusedly. "Don't you have any two-syllable words in your vocabulary?"

He was trying to be kind. She understood that, but she didn't want any more trouble than she already had. She stared toward the house, hating the rain that imprisoned her here with Ted.

He saw her impatience to leave and it angered him out of all proportion.

"Damn it!" he burst out.

Her face jerked toward his. Her eyes were enormous, frightened.

"Oh, for God's sake," he groaned. "I've never hit a woman in my life! I lose my temper from time to time. I'm impatient and when things upset me, I say so. That doesn't mean I'm going to hurt you, honey!"

The endearment went through her as if it were electricity. He'd never once used an endearment when they spoke. She'd never even heard him use them to Sandy. Her eyes dropped, embarrassed.

He looked at her openly, curious, astonished at her reaction to what had been an involuntary slip of the tongue.

He moved a step closer, slowly, so that he wouldn't alarm her. She looked up, but she didn't back away. He stopped an arm's length from her, because that was when she tensed. His pale eyes wandered over her face and from the distance, he could see the deep hollows in it, the shadows under her eyes.

"You don't sleep at all, do you?" he asked gently.

"There's been so much," she faltered. "You can't imagine—"

"I think I can," he interrupted bluntly. "Coreen, I think some therapy would be a good idea. You must have realized that a warped relationship can damage you emotionally."

"I'm not ready for that now," she said evenly. "I'm tired and I hurt all over. I just want to rest and not have to think about things that disturb me." She drew in a long, weary breath. Her hand went to her short hair and toyed with a strand of it beside her flushed cheek. "I know you don't want me here, Ted. Why won't you let me go to Victoria and stay with Sandy?"

His jutting chin raised and one eye narrowed. "Who says I won't?"

"Sandy. She said you kept finding excuses why we can't use the apartment."

"They're not excuses," he said. "They're reasons. Good reasons."

Her thin shoulders rose and fell impotently.

"You'd be alone during the day, when Sandy's working," he explained quietly. "At least I'm somewhere nearby when she's gone, or Mrs. Bird is."

"You aren't responsible for me."

"Yes, I am," he said. "I'm responsible for the trust Barry left you. That makes you my concern."

"Oh, I don't want the money," she said wearily, turning away. "Money was never why I married him!"

"The money is yours," he argued. "And you'll take it, all right."

Her head came up. For an instant he thought he'd found the spark he'd been looking for, a way to bring her out of her shell and back into the world. But the spark died even as he watched.

"I don't feel like fighting," she said. "When I'm back on my feet, I'll find a job and a place to stay. Then I'll be out of your hair for good."

That was what he was afraid of. He wanted to talk to her, to explain how he felt, but the rain began to fall more slowly, and the instant it lessened to a sprinkle Coreen was out of the stable and on her way to the house as if pack dogs were nipping at her heels.

Chapter Six

"He's so restless lately, have you noticed?" Sandy asked Coreen one afternoon when Ted was working on a truck with two of his men. "I've never heard him use language like that within earshot of the house."

The language was audible, all right. Coreen peeked out the window toward the metal building where the ranch vehicles were kept. One of the men with Ted had thrown down a wrench and he was stomping off in disgust.

"Hawkins, get back here or get another job!" Ted yelled after him.

"I'll get another job, then!" came the angry reply. "Can't be worse than this!"

"Coward!" the third man called after him gleefully.

"Do you want to go with him, Charlie?" Ted asked with a dangerous smile.

Charlie picked up the dropped wrench and offered it to the greasy man bending over the engine of the truck.

Coreen was shivering. Angry voices still made her uneasy, and Ted was much more volatile than she'd ever realized. At home, without any social restraints on his temper, it seemed to be terrible.

"How do you stand it?" Coreen asked Sandy nervously, as they set the table.

Sandy stopped what she was doing and turned to her friend, hardly aware of a cessation of the noise outside. "He isn't like Barry," she said softly. "He isn't a violent man. It takes a lot to make him fight, and he doesn't hit women. He's just upset because he's been unkind to you, and that's why he's being impossible to live with. He's sorry about the way he's treated you and too proud to apologize for it."

"He's very loud," Coreen muttered.

"He's a marshmallow inside" came the musing reply. "What you see isn't the real man. Ted hides what he feels under that prickly exterior. It keeps people from finding out how vulnerable he really is."

"In a pig's eye," Coreen retorted. "He's steel right through."

Sandy put a plate down a little noisily. "But you don't hate him," she added, her voice as clear as a bell in the room.

Coreen flushed. She started to argue, aware of Sandy's level stare and a tiny flicker of diverted attention that was quickly concealed.

"Do you?" she persisted.

"No," Coreen confessed, her eyes lowered. "But it might have been easier for me if I had, once. Barry made my life so miserable. You can't imagine what it's like to have someone taunt you with feelings you can't help, to hold another man's rejection over your head for years, reminding you over and over again that you weren't worth loving. He was so jealous of Ted... insanely jealous, even though he didn't really want me himself. He couldn't stand it when he found out how I felt about Ted. I think he would have killed me, that last night..."

A faint sound from behind her brought her head around. Ted had been standing in the open doorway. His face was hard and drawn, oddly pale.

"Well, get an earful, Ted," Coreen muttered with the first show of spirit yet. An open sack of flour sat on the table beside her and she accidentally knocked it with her elbow, jumping to catch it before it fell. Even then she fumbled and had to clutch it to her.

"Miss Graceful," Ted drawled without thinking.

To Coreen, it was the last straw. She could see the sudden recognition, the regret, in Ted's face as he remembered too late what Harry had told them about Barry taunting her with her clumsiness. But her self-control was gone. It was one taunt too many.

She didn't even think. She wheeled and threw the bag of flour at him without a single hesitation.

The bag was made of paper and it broke immediately. Ted's shocked expression was coated in a white layer of flour, like the whole front of him. It mingled with the grease to give him a vaguely mottled look.

"Tarred and feathered," Sandy remarked pleasantly and suddenly broke into gales of laughter.

Ted glared at her and then Coreen, who was as shocked by her own actions as Ted seemed to be.

Coreen saw the flash of anger in his pale eyes and the color that overlaid his cheekbones as he stared at her. She felt sick all over, remembering how Barry had reacted if she showed any spirit at all. She felt her knees shaking as she stared up at Ted, waiting for the explosion, waiting for him to hit her.

That expression in her eyes stopped Ted's anger cold. He calmed down at once. "For a woman who hates violence," he remarked through floury lips, "you have an absolutely *amazing* lack of restraint."

With a rueful smile, he turned and left a white trail behind him on his way out of the kitchen.

"And let that be a lesson to you!" Sandy yelled after him. "Never make a woman mad when she's cooking!"

The cowboy who was helping him must have been standing on the front porch, because there was a cry of dismay followed by such howling laughter that muttered curses echoed from the hall.

Coreen was devastated by what she'd done. She was even more devastated by the fact that Ted hadn't retaliated. It was such a relief that she started crying. Sandy hugged her, fighting her own amusement. "Now, now, he won't die from a coating of flour. Listen, Coreen, listen, if he doesn't get it all off, we can toss him in the pan and fry him up nice and toasty. He's already covered with grease and now he's properly battered..."

Coreen felt the tears turn to laughter at the thought of a crispy Ted lying on a big platter.

Ted was cleaned up when he came to supper. He glared at both women, but he didn't say a word about what had happened.

Coreen ate with a little more appetite than she'd had. She and Barry had rarely eaten together, except when they were first married. And that had only been so that he could torment her about Ted.

When they progressed to dessert, Ted picked up his second cup of coffee and walked out of the room without a word.

"He's in a snit," Sandy remarked. "But he'll regret leaving that cake behind. Why don't you take it to him and make up?"

"I don't want to make up."

"Yes, you do." Sandy smiled at her. "Go on. It won't hurt."

"That's what you think. You knew he was standing there, didn't you?"

Sandy flushed. "I only wanted him to know that you didn't hate him. I thought it might help. I'm sorry."

Coreen didn't answer. She got up and took the dish of cake to the room Ted used as a study. The door wasn't closed. He was sitting behind his big oak desk staring blankly at the opposite wall with his coffee cup perched on one big hand.

"Didn't you want any cake?" Coreen asked hesitantly.

He leaned back in the chair, still with the coffee cup in his hand, and stared at her. "Sandy sent you, didn't she?" He laughed when her expression gave her away. "I didn't think you'd come of your own accord."

She moved into the room, ignoring the sarcastic remark, and put his cake on the desk.

"I didn't mean to say what I did," he said quietly. "I know that you aren't normally a clumsy woman. It was a slip of the tongue that I regretted the minute I made it."

"And I overreacted," she confessed. She traced the grain of the wood on his desk. "I'm sorry, too." She glanced up. "You didn't try to hit me."

His face went rigid. "I don't have to beat up a woman to feel like a man."

"It's nice to know for sure, though."

He could understand how she might feel that way. He didn't like thinking about it. He sipped his coffee and put the cup on the desk, watching her with a faint smile. "I don't suppose you might like to kiss and make up?" he asked unexpectedly.

Her shocked eyes met his.

"Oh, nothing heavy," he clarified. His eyes were watchful, but teasing and oddly tender. "It would do you good, to be kissed in a way that wouldn't hurt you or scar you."

"I don't ever want to be that close to a man again," she said miserably.

"Sure you feel that way, now," he returned, his voice still soft. "But it isn't natural to let it continue. It would be a pity to waste those maternal instincts you used to have. Do you remember when Mary Gibbs brought her baby into your father's store, Coreen?" he added wistfully, as if the memory was one he cherished. "You'd stand there and hold that little boy, and your face would glow."

"But, you never saw me . . ." she began.

His eyes lifted to hers. "I never stopped seeing you," he replied bluntly. "I watched you all the time, even when you didn't know I was around. My God, honey, you still don't understand, do you?"

She shook her head.

"I'm forty years old," he said softly. "You're barely twenty-four."

She just looked at him. It still didn't register, and her eyes told him so.

He let out a rough sigh. "I'm sixteen years older than you are," he said heavily. "You don't realize, you can't realize, what a burden that age difference would become."

Her eyes slid over his lean, tanned face. "I'm nothing to you," she said simply. "So what difference does it make? I don't hate you, but I don't love you, either. You made sure of that. You're safe, Ted," she added without expression. "I'll never be a threat to you, or any other man, ever again."

She turned and started out of the room. She hadn't even heard him move when she saw his arm slide past her and push the office door shut with a hard snap.

Too nervous to turn, she hesitated. He had her by both shoulders all at once, and the next minute, she was standing with her back to the door and a furious Ted towering over her.

"Which doesn't mean that I'm not a threat to you," he replied with glittery pale blue eyes. "I'm so damned tired of being noble...!"

He bent and moved his mouth square over hers with an economy of motion that left her no time to anticipate it.

She gasped under the warm, hard crush of his lips and her hands went automatically to his shirtfront to push.

He lifted his mouth just enough to allow speech, but when he spoke, his lips were still touching hers. "I'm not going to hurt you," he said tenderly. "Not in any way at all. I'm not even going to hold you. Try not to fight me, sweetheart. Just this once, let me kiss you."

It would be fatal. She knew it. But the sweet pressure of his mouth on hers was nectar. It had been years, and she'd loved him so much. Their time had already passed, but this tiny space of seconds was like a reminder of what could have been.

She didn't fight. Her lips brushed against his in a slow, gentle glide that became, eventually, insistent and deep. But he didn't hold her or imprison her. Only their lips touched, for seconds that seemed endless.

When he finally lifted his head, she was breathless.

His pale eyes searched hers solemnly. "That's how it could have been," he said huskily. "And even that is just the beginning."

She managed to shake off her languor and shook her head. "Don't torment me, Ted," she whispered bitterly.

He scowled. "Torment you?"

"I can't go through it again," she whispered, wincing. "He tormented me with you. He told me what you said when you came to visit us," she added, looking up with anguished eyes. "That you'd only played with me before I married him, that you'd never wanted me anyway, because I was so thin and boyish, that I wasn't woman enough..."

His eyes closed. "Coreen..."

She pulled away from him and opened the door.

"It wasn't true," he said roughly.

She looked at him over her shoulder. "But, it was," she said sadly. "You told me so yourself, that night at the dance."

"I lied," he said bitingly.

She smiled sadly. "It's all right, Ted. It was all a long time ago. But don't...don't try to make me care for you again. We both know that you have...new interests, now."

She was gone before he made the connection. Lillian. She thought he was involved with Lillian. He could have cursed himself for bringing the woman here in the first place. He'd fouled up everything. Coreen wouldn't let him near her. She'd believed Barry. She thought Ted was only playing. For a minute, he felt total despair. There had to be a way, some way, to show her that things were different now. He just didn't know how.

As it turned out, Topper was the bait that lured Coreen out of the house. She enjoyed watching the trainer work the young filly on the track out behind the house. While she watched Topper, Ted watched her.

She was blooming here, with no one to hurt her or torment her. Day by day, her complexion turned rosy and she began to smile. Her blue eyes lit like fireflies and she began to gain a little weight as well.

She was standing on the lower rail of the track, watching Topper run, when she felt Ted behind her. She didn't have to turn and look. She knew when he was close by. It was like intuition.

"The sun's hot," he said, lifting her down by the waist. "Don't stay out here too long."

"Oh, Ted, don't fuss, I'm having...oh!"

When she turned, the bandage around his arm shocked her speechless. It was bloody, but he looked amused at her horror.

"Bull gored me, that's all," he mused. "Nothing to worry about."

Her hands trembled as she touched the bandage. "It hasn't even stopped bleeding! Come on." He didn't budge. She caught him by his good arm, her face contorted with worry. "Ted, come on! Please!"

He let her drag him into the house through the back door that led into the kitchen. She held his arm over the sink and unwrapped the makeshift bandage. There was too much blood even to see the damage, and thank goodness she wasn't squeamish.

She bathed the wound very gently, and then held pressure over it, wincing at the pain she must be causing him. But after two minutes, the bleeding hadn't stopped.

She looked up into his eyes worriedly. "It's cut a vein," she said. "It won't stop bleeding. You have to go to the doctor!"

He smiled gently at her. "Coreen, I've been gored before," he began. "I know what to do."

Her jaw set. "I'm taking you to the doctor, Ted, you might as well stop arguing because I'll call an ambulance if you don't."

He opened his mouth to argue, but the paleness of her complexion and the wild look in her eyes stopped him. It touched him deeply that she was that concerned. And he liked the new show of spirit. She'd been subdued for so long now that he'd despaired of her strength ever returning.

"All right, Corrie," he said, using the familiar nickname for the first time since she'd been here.

She didn't notice. She was terrified that he was going to bleed to death. If only Sandy or Mrs. Bird was here! She had no one to help her.

Ted dug out his truck keys and handed them to her. "Can you handle it? It's a long bed."

"Yes, I can drive," she muttered, herding him toward the big red-and-white truck. "And I won't back it into a barn or a ditch."

He chuckled. "Okay."

For a man who was bleeding to death, he certainly was cheerful! She got him into the truck and climbed in under the wheel, demanding the name and address of his doctor.

She didn't falter all the way to town. Her eyes kept shifting worriedly to the soaked towel around his forearm, but he was amazingly unconcerned. Just as well, she thought; she was frightened enough for both of them.

At the doctor's office, she led him inside and gave his name to the receptionist, who knew Ted and smothered a grin at the sight of him being led around by this small, determined woman.

But when she noticed the way he was bleeding, she called the nurse and got them right into an examination room. Dr. Lou Blakely came in, wearing a white coat and a grin on her pretty face.

"You're Dr. Lou Blakely?" Coreen asked.

The willowy blond woman chuckled as she began to examine Ted's wound. "Lou is short for Louise," she explained. "What happened to you, Ted?"

"A bad-tempered bull. She wouldn't rest until she dragged me here," he muttered good-naturedly, nodding toward Coreen.

"She did the right thing," Lou said, frowning. "You'll need stitches. How about your tetanus booster?"

"Current," he said. "Barely."

"You'll need another. Betty!" she called to her nurse. "Bring some sutures and iodine and a tetanus hypodermic, will you, while I check on Mr. Bailey in room three?"

"Right away" came the reply.

"I'll be back in a minute," Lou promised, stepping down the hall.

"You can wait outside if you'd rather not watch," Ted told Coreen, who was sitting stiffly in a chair by the examination table.

She looked up, her face almost tragic. Tears rolled down her cheeks. "If you want me to..."

He let out a sharp breath. "Corrie!" He held out his good hand and she took it. Her lower lip trembled. "Oh, honey!" he whispered huskily, his eyes glittery with feeling. "Honey, don't cry! I'm all right!"

"It's bleeding so," she whispered brokenly.

He pulled her head to his chest and pressed it there, overcome by tenderness. Tears in her eyes affected him violently. His hand contracted in her hair. "I'm all right!" he said huskily.

Lou and the nurse entered together and Coreen had to let go of Ted while they worked.

Lou smiled at Coreen. "He's tougher than he looks. Honest."

Coreen nodded, not trusting her voice.

They finished, finally, and Coreen went out with the nurse, Betty, while Lou gave the tetanus booster to Ted.

"How long have you been married?" Betty asked, oblivious to the fact that Coreen was wearing Barry's wedding band, not Ted's.

"Oh, I, uh..."

"Not long enough," Ted replied, sliding an arm around her shoulders. "Come on, baby, I'll take you home. Thanks, Betty."

"Sure thing, Mr. Regan."

"You let her think we were married," Coreen protested when they reached the truck.

"Betty's new here. And explanations take too long." He paused at the passenger door and looked down at her with quiet, soft eyes. "You're still wearing his wedding band. Why?"

She twisted it on her finger. "I thought if I took it off, you'd think it was one more black mark against me," she said with resignation.

He caught her hand and wrenched the ring off, glaring at it. He dropped it in the sand and ground it under his heel, staring into Coreen's shocked eyes.

"But..."

He bent and put his mouth over hers in a brief, hard kiss. "Drive me home."

He got into the truck and closed the door. She hesitated, looking down at where the ring had been. But she didn't try to pick it up. Whatever had been, her marriage was a thing of the past. She had to put it out of sight, like the wedding ring that signified it. Was that what Ted had meant with the gesture?

She drove the truck back to the ranch, silent and thoughtful.

When Sandy returned from work, she was astonished at Ted's refusal to see a doctor without prodding.

"You idiot," she fumed at him over supper. "I try to save you from lung cancer by hiding your cigarettes and here you go trying to get tetanus! Thank goodness Corrie was here!"

He was watching Coreen. "Yes," he agreed. "Thank goodness she was."

Sandy put down her fork and sipped her hot tea. "Ted, have you checked on the apartment for me?" she asked.

He lowered his eyes to his plate and toyed with a bit of steak. "I haven't had time, Sandy. I'll get around to it in a day or so."

Sandy glanced toward Coreen and rolled her eyes.

"You know very well that Corrie doesn't need to be on her own all day while you work," Ted said surprisingly. "At least she's properly looked after here."

"I'm much better," Coreen protested. "I don't hurt nearly as much when I move around, and I'm not dizzy."

"You're still in a state of shock, though," he replied. "You've been through a lot. Too much," he added shortly.

"He's right," Sandy agreed. "You aren't really unhappy here, are you Corrie?"

There was a hesitation. Coreen glanced shyly at Ted. "I like watching the trainer with Topper," she confessed. "If I move to Victoria, I'd miss that."

They both smiled. "You'll stay, then," Ted said.

"Yes, thank you, for now. But I should be able to get a job soon," Coreen added slowly. "And find a place of my own."

Ted put down his fork and glared at her. "What's wrong with staying here?"

"But I can't," she told him. "Ted, I'm not part of the family, I'm a financial burden you've assumed until I reach twenty-five. You don't have to..."

"Oh, hell, I know I don't have to," he muttered. "Have you thought about what you're qualified to do? And how much strength it's going to require, working an eight-hour day? And what it will cost, even in Jacobsville, to rent rooms?"

She'd tried not to think about her situation. It showed in her face.

"It's a big house," he coaxed. "Sandy and I are all alone here. You're company for her, the best friend she has."

"But..."

"Corrie, just get well," he said gently. "You've got an allowance from the legacy that will more than take care of your odds and ends until you're completely well. Don't think about tomorrow. There's plenty of time for that."

"Listen to him, will you?" Sandy said, smiling. "Honestly, I'll go crazy if you leave now."

"If I'm not in the way," she faltered.

Everyone knew that meant "yes." Ted started eating again, and his smile betrayed just a little smugness.

The trainer was an elderly man who'd worked with thoroughbreds all his life. He had a son named Barney who came to visit on weekends, and who noticed Coreen very quickly. He was a sweet-natured man, not terribly educated, but kind. She warmed to Barney quickly and began to spend time with him when he came on the weekends to visit his father.

The problem began when Ted started spending more time at home and noticed the amount of contact Coreen was having with his trainer's closest relation. He didn't like it, and he stopped it. Coreen missed Barney and asked his father why he hadn't come back.

He told her that Ted had arranged a nice job for his son, and that Barney was over the moon about it. But Coreen wondered if it had been a benevolent gesture on Ted's part or something more. It didn't occur to her that he might be jealous; she simply saw it as one more way he'd found to get at her.

She had to know, so she went looking for him that same morning. She found him in his office, talking on the telephone. She started to back out, but he gestured impatiently for her to come in.

He was giving somebody hell over the telephone. He finished with a curt demand and hung up before the person at the other end of the line had time for any outcry.

"Well?" he demanded, and the leftover anger in his pale eyes made her stand very still.

Chapter Seven

Ted saw her apprehension and forced himself to calm down. He leaned back in his swivel chair with his hands behind his head and stared at her patiently. "What can I do for you?" he asked.

She hesitated. "Barney's Dad said that you found him a job in Victoria."

He nodded slowly, and began to look more unapproachable. His silver hair caught the light and glittered like metal. "So?"

She didn't know how to answer that. She wanted to ask if he'd sent Barney away deliberately because she was spending so much time with him, but that might sound as if she were accusing him of being jealous. Heaven knew, she didn't think that was the reason!

"Go ahead," he invited.

Her eyebrows arched. "Go ahead and do what?"

"Ask me if I did it to keep him away from here."

She folded her hands in front of her. "Did you?" she asked.

His pale eyes in one glance took in her body in its pale pink short-sleeved knit top and close-fitting jeans. She was gaining a little weight, and she looked pretty. "What?" he murmured absently, distracted.

"I asked if you sent Barney away because he was spending so much time with me."

His eyes narrowed and grew cold as they levered back up to meet hers. "As a matter of fact, I did."

Her lips parted on a expelled breath. "Oh. I see."

"Do you?" he replied. He leaned forward suddenly and got to his feet. "You might remember that I hired his father, not him."

"You don't have to justify yourself," she said in a subdued tone as she turned away. Bitter memories intruded on the present, and her voice was almost absent as she murmured, "Anything that I like has to go, doesn't it, even people? Barry once had a dog shot because I stroked it—"

She was stopped in midsentence by the steely lean hand that caught her arm and spun her around. She gasped at the suddenness of the action. Nor did he let her go when he had her standing stock-still.

"I didn't have the damned man shot, I got him a good job," he said through his teeth, and his pale eyes were flashing dangerously at her. "I do nothing to deliberately hurt you! Stop tarring me with the same brush you used on my cousin."

His anger was intimidating. He was like a summer storm in anger, all flashing fury. But she remembered when she'd thrown the flour at him and he hadn't retaliated. He could control his temper. Barry had never tried.

His other hand caught her by the waist, lightly, and held her when she would have pulled back. His gaze was curious now, speculative.

"Sandy says you're afraid of me," he asked bluntly. "Are you?"

She lowered her eyes to his chest, and she watched its regular rise and fall. "You're... volatile."

"I've always been volatile," he returned. "Hot tempers run in my family. But I've told you before that I don't attack women."

"I know that. Not even when you're drowned in flour," she added with a faint smile.

He tilted her face up to his, and she expected to find humor in his eyes. But she didn't. He was solemn, searching her wan face with intent curiosity.

"You were telling Sandy that Barry taunted you with me..."

She pushed at him. "Please, don't!"

"No, Coreen, I'm not trying to embarrass you," he said gently. He stilled her uncoordinated movements. "Listen, he was playing both ends against the middle. He told me that I was the reason you couldn't bear for him to touch you."

"That wasn't true." She couldn't look at him. "I never felt anything with him, physically, except fear and pain. It had nothing to do with you."

"It made me feel guilty all the same," he returned abruptly. "When Barry was young, he was my shadow. He always seemed to look on me as a father figure after his own father died."

"He envied you," she replied. "You were everything he wanted to be, and never could. He . . . said once that he wanted me because he thought you did. It was like a contest for him, taking something you prized away from you." She laughed bitterly. "Funny, isn't it? He married me and then found out that you didn't want me at all."

"And made you pay for it?"

She shivered. "I don't want to talk about it, Ted."

He drew in an angry breath, staring over her head toward the wall. Her comment about the dog Barry had ordered shot gave him even more unwanted insight into what her married life had been like. He hated what he was seeing.

"It's all over now," she said after a minute. His nearness was disturbing to her. She drew back from him and he let her go, but his eyes still held her, filled with turmoil, with emotions she couldn't read.

"Did Sandy ever tell you about our father and mother?" he asked hesitantly.

She nodded. "Many times."

He ran a lean hand through his silver hair. "The age difference between them destroyed their marriage. Eventually he couldn't keep up with her in the social whirl she liked. She started going out alone, left him behind. It was inevitable that she'd fall in love with someone closer to her own age and leave him, but he couldn't see it. He grieved all his life for her, and Sandy and I paid for that. He blamed us because she left him. He said that if it hadn't been for him wanting kids, she'd still be with him."

She winced at his tone, and her heart ached for the little boy he once was. It must have hurt him terribly to overhear such things. "Oh, Ted, if it hadn't been you and Sandy it would have been some other excuse. She couldn't have loved him enough, don't you see? If she had, she'd have been home with him, not going to parties! She wouldn't have wanted to go anywhere without him!"

He turned and looked at her, his eyes narrow and assessive. "Is that your definition of a happy marriage? Two people who are inseparable?"

"Two people with common interests," she corrected, "who love each other but are kind to each other and want the same things from life." She shrugged helplessly. "Barry wanted bright lights and alcohol and beautiful companions. He liked people with his same sort of intolerance for differences and his pleasure-oriented attitude toward life. I don't like social occasions at all. I like being outdoors and I love animals." She folded her arms over her breasts. "He wouldn't even let me have a goldfish in the house."

He felt as if he'd never known one single thing about her as she said that. She liked the outdoors, liked animals . . . of course she did; she'd spent plenty of time at the ranch before she married Barry. She loved horses and riding and she'd never been one for parties. Why hadn't he noticed? She even liked skeet shooting, or she had before he'd made it impossible for her to go to the gun club with her father.

His tormented look puzzled her. She studied him curiously.

"I never knew you," he said slowly.

"You never wanted to," she replied flatly. She sighed and turned away. "And what does it matter now, anyway, Ted?"

She had her hand on the doorknob when he spoke.

"If Barney's company means that much to you, I'll withdraw the job offer," he said bitterly.

She didn't look back. "No, it's...he's very happy, his father said. He was just being friendly, Ted, that's all. You and Sandy have been very kind to me. It's just that..." How could she tell him that she was alone too much, that she needed someone to talk to? Sandy had to work and so did he. Besides, it would sound as if she was begging him to keep her company. "Never mind."

"Are you lonely, Coreen?" he asked softly.

Her hand tightened on the doorknob. She drew in a slow breath. "Aren't most people?" she asked in a haunted tone. She opened the door and went out.

Coreen was surprised to find Ted at the table the next morning when she went to eat breakfast. Sandy had said that she'd have to leave very early for an appointment in Houston, and Coreen had given herself the luxury of sleeping late. It was after ten when she dressed in jeans and a floppy knit blouse and went in search of toast and coffee.

She stopped in the doorway, staring at Ted.

"Sleepyhead," he chided kindly. "Sit down and eat."

"It's after ten," she commented.

"Oh, I had something to do this morning," he said mysteriously. He poured her a cup of coffee and put it at her place, pushing the milk and sugar toward her. "Nibble on something and then I've got a surprise for you."

Her eyes widened. "For me?"

He nodded. His pale eyes twinkled. "No, I'm not going to tell you yet. Eat up."

She hadn't had many pleasant surprises. She ate a piece of toast and drank her coffee, all the while watching Ted intently for any giveaway expression. It wasn't like him to give presents, except to Sandy.

"Through?" he commented when she dabbed at her unvarnished lips. "Okay. Come on."

He led her through the kitchen, calling a greeting to Mrs. Bird on the way through. They went out to the stable and she looked up at him curiously as he stopped at the first stall and opened it to let her in.

Curled up on a soft cloth in the stall was a baby collie. Coreen could hardly breathe as she looked at it.

She went down on her knees beside the little thing. It opened its eyes and made tiny whimpering sounds. She gathered it up in her arms and cuddled it, laughing when it licked her chin. Tears of joy and gratitude and surprise rolled soundlessly down her cheeks.

Ted knelt beside her. "He's a beaut, isn't he? He's already been to the vet for his shots and checkup. He's purebred, too, you'll have to name him...Corrie!" he exclaimed when he saw the tears, shocked speechless.

"Thank you." She choked out the words, smiling up at him. "Oh, thank you, Ted, he's the most beautiful...thing...!" Impulsively she reached up to pull his face down and she kissed him enthusiastically on his hard mouth.

Then, embarrassed, she pulled back at once and turned her attention to the puppy. "I'll call him Shep," she whispered huskily. "Isn't he gorgeous?"

Ted was silent. His pale eyes were riveted to her bent head and he was scowling. He wondered if she even realized what she'd done. The impulse that had led him in search of the puppy made him feel good. It was the first spark of pleasure he'd seen her betray since she'd been here.

"Well, I can see that I won't get another sensible word out of you today. I've got to go to work." He got up.

Coreen stood up, too, clutching her puppy. "Why?" she asked breathlessly.

He touched her mouth with his forefinger. "Maybe I like seeing you happy."

"Thank you. I'll take ever such good care of him."

He smiled. "Sure you will." He withdrew his hand and left her to it.

Sandy was fascinated by the puppy. She was more fascinated by the fact that Ted had bought it for Coreen.

"He's never wanted animals around, except for the horses and the cattle dogs he uses on the beef property," Sandy explained. "He'd have let me have pets, if I'd wanted to, but he's never been much of an animal lover—well, except for the horses," she repeated. She frowned. "Curious, isn't it, that he'd buy you a dog."

"I don't understand it, either," Coreen confessed. "But isn't he a beautiful dog?"

"Indeed he is. My, my, isn't my brother a mass of contradictions." She sighed.

Coreen and the puppy were inseparable after that. He followed her on her walks and laid in the corner while she helped Mrs. Bird in the kitchen. She bathed him and combed him, careful not to hurt him where he'd had his shots from the vet. She doted on him, and vice versa.

When she went to ask Ted about some paperwork Sandy had mentioned he needed help with, Shep came trotting along at her heels.

"My God, the terrible twins," Ted drawled when they walked into his study, but he was smiling when he said it.

"Isn't he cute?" She chuckled. The puppy had already made a world of difference in her. His vulnerability brought out all her protective instincts, as Sandy had already related.

"I hear you're fighting his battles already," he mentioned.

She flushed. "Well, it was a vicious big dog. I couldn't let him hurt Shep."

"What was it you threw at him?" he asked. "A handful of eggs, wasn't it?"

She flushed even more and then glared at him. "Well, they scared him off, didn't they?"

"And I didn't get my chocolate cake for dessert because they were the last eggs Mrs. Bird had, and she didn't have a way to get to the store to buy more," he added.

"Oh, Ted, I'm sorry! I didn't know!"

He laughed at her expression. "I can live without chocolate cake for one more day. You threw flour at me and eggs at the invading dog—I guess it'll be milk cartons you'll be heaving next." He pursed his lips. "Talk about mixing up cake the hard way...!"

"Stop making nasty remarks about me or I'll sic Shep on you," she threatened.

The puppy waddled over to him and began licking his outstretched hand. He gave her a speaking glance.

She glared harder. "Traitor," she told Shep.

"Little things like me," he commented, and his face softened as he looked at the dog.

"Haven't you ever wanted children?" she asked without thinking.

His eyes came up and met hers and then suddenly dropped to her waistline and lingered there for so long that she felt hot all over. Her lips parted. Her body responded to that look in ways she hadn't dreamed it could. She stared at him breathlessly while his hot gaze levered back up to her mouth and then to her shocked eyes.

"Are you reading my mind already?" he asked tautly when he saw her expression.

She couldn't find an answer that wouldn't incriminate her. He got up from the chair, slowly, holding her gaze as he walked carefully around the puppy and stopped just in front of her, so close that she could feel the heat of his body and the soft whip of his breath on her temple.

"I've never let myself want a child," he said roughly. "Do you know why?"

She barely had the strength to shake her head.

"Because people would mistake me for its grandfather. I'm feeling my years a bit, Corrie. I wouldn't be able to do all the things children like doing with their parents. By the time a child of mine was ready for college, I'd be almost ready for Social Security."

Her blue eyes sought his and searched his lean, dark face. "You're so handsome," she said involuntarily. "It would ... be a pity not to have a child of your own."

His heartbeat went wild. He'd never felt such desire for a woman. He reached out and touched her throat, where a pulse shuddered just under the skin.

"Thinking about children excites you," he commented roughly. "Did you want one of your own?"

"Not with him," she said, her voice unsteady. "I made sure that I couldn't."

His hand stilled at her throat. "What do you mean, you made sure?" he demanded.

There was a note to his voice, an urgency, that was disturbing. She searched his worried eyes. "I mean, I took something to prevent a child," she said.

He let out a breath that he hadn't realized he was holding. "You didn't have surgery?"

"Oh, no," she said. His eyes disturbed her. "Why would it bother you to think that I couldn't have a child?" she blurted out, and then stood still with horror at what she'd asked so blatantly.

If she'd shocked herself, it seemed that she'd shocked him even more. He stared at her blankly for a moment. Then he scowled and searched her eyes until she flushed.

"I don't know," he said honestly. He moved closer, bringing his hands up to frame her oval face. They were faintly callused hands, warm and strong against her skin.

Her fascinated eyes fell to his mouth and she remembered how it had felt the morning he gave her Shep, when she'd kissed him so uninhibitedly.

His hands tilted her head just a little, and one thumb eased up to her lower lip, teasing it to part from her top one.

"Keep your eyes open while I kiss you," he said huskily, bending slowly toward her. "I want you to know who I am, every minute!"

As if she could forget, she thought with faint hysteria. His hard mouth parted against hers, his lips easing down on hers with a slow, sensuous pressure.

She stiffened and her hands went to his shirt, but he didn't stop.

His hand came up to stroke her cheek, toy with her mouth while his lips explored it. And all the while he watched her watching him, seeing her pupils begin to dilate when his body shifted against her, dragging her breasts against his broad chest.

His free hand slid down her back to the base of her spine and gathered her sinuously against him, so that she felt his jean-clad thigh push between her own legs in an intimacy that was new and exciting.

He lifted his head to look at her. His breathing was as unsteady as her own, and there was nothing calm in his eyes now. He traced her cheek and the outline of her mouth. At the same time, his muscular leg moved farther between hers and his hand pressed her closer in a new and disturbing intimacy. She could feel the insistent pressure of him against the inside of her thigh. It was the first time since she'd first met him that he'd ever allowed her to feel his body in complete arousal.

She started to pull back instinctively, but he moved so that he was perched against the edge of his desk. He drew her in between his legs and held her there by both hips, deliberately moving her to make her aware of what he was feeling.

She blushed and her eyes couldn't get higher than his chin.

"Look at me, Corrie," he said huskily.

She had to drag her eyes up, and they were shy, apprehensive, excited all at once.

His lips parted on a slowly released breath, and his hands lifted her slightly into an even more intimate position. He caught his breath sharply at the sensations it brought and his teeth clenched. He held her there firmly, groaning softly with pleasure at her involuntary movement.

"Ted . . . !" she protested in a feverish whisper.

"I'd like to make you feel the kind of pleasure it gives me to hold you like this, Corrie," he said, staring into her eyes. He smiled gently. "Embarrassed?"

"I've never done this with you," she faltered.

"No," he agreed. His eyes fell to her soft knit blouse and lingered where her nipples pressed visibly against the cloth.

She knew what he was looking for. Her own body was her worst enemy, but she couldn't hide it from him.

One long leg came around her legs at the knee, holding her, while his hand slid under the knit top. He caught her eyes and slowly lifted his hand under the hem until it reached the thin garment that was no barrier to his touch. He traced the nipple with his forefinger and thumb and felt her whole body jerk.

"Is this where he cut you?" he asked very quietly.

She swallowed. "No. It's . . . the other one," she whispered.

"I'll be very careful with you," he promised softly. "Don't be frightened."

He reached around behind her and unfastened the catch. Seconds later, his hand pressed tenderly against her bareness and she gasped at the sensations he drew from her body so effortlessly.

His hands slid up her rib cage, taking the fabric with them, and when she caught them, he only shook his head and kept going.

The impact of his eyes on her bare flesh made her very still. He studied the long, thin scar with the tracks of removed stitches still visible, and his jaw tautened. Then his attention turned to her other breast and lingered there for a long moment on the perfection of it, the firm, creamy softness with its hard, dusky tip.

When she saw his head bend, she was too hypnotized to register what it meant. Then his mouth opened on her unblemished breast and began to suckle her. She stiffened and clutched at him, making a tiny cry in her throat.

He drew back at once to see whether passion or fear had produced that choked sound.

"Am I hurting you?" he asked softly.

She bit her lower lip, hesitating as she tried to decide between the truth and a lie.

But he knew. A warm light darkened his pale eyes. "Don't be embarrassed," he said softly. "I'm enjoying it, too. You're so soft, Corrie. It's like rubbing my lips over a rose petal."

He bent again, and this time she had no resistance left. She gave in to him without a protest, moaning softly as he suckled her until she trembled, totally given over to the delicious sensations he was creating.

She felt him lift her, turn her, so that she was suddenly lying back on the desk among the papers and pens. His mouth was insistent, demanding, and she felt his hand on her inner thigh, parting her legs. He lowered his hips against hers. The blatant feel of him in intimacy, even through two layers of denim, was explosive. She cried out and lifted helplessly upward, straining against him, while one lean hand snaked under her and pulled her into him with a quick, hard rhythm.

Her nails dug into his shoulders and she shivered, moaning so hungrily that his mouth left her breast to grind into her own and silence her. She shivered again, her hands urgent, clinging, pulling, in a delirium of anguished hunger.

He was as far gone as she was, totally without restraint. Ignoring the clutter of the desk, he pressed her down into it with the weight of his body and drove against her with a harsh, blind groan of pleasure.

She hadn't realized what could happen, even when two people were fully clothed. She bit his lower lip ardently, tugged at his thick silver hair, moved under him with wanton little jerks until the pleasure made her shake all over. She wept because it wasn't enough, and there was no possibility of getting any closer to him.

He realized belatedly how far they were going. His breath left him in a rough explosion, and for an instant his hands were cruel as he fought for control.

"Help me," he whispered into her open, ardent mouth. "Help me, Corrie. Lie still, honey, please...!"

She sobbed brokenly under his mouth while he soothed and gentled her until passion slowly gave way to exhaustion and her body stopped shivering.

Finally her eyes opened. The ceiling was above her and she felt paper clips under her shoulders and what felt like a pencil against her jean-clad hip. Seconds later, Ted's pale, hard face lifted and his turbulent pale blue eyes looked into hers.

She felt as shocked as he looked, and a lot more embarrassed.

"Easy now," he said softly. "It's all right." He lifted himself away from her and moved off the side of the huge desk, his eyes on the disorder they'd created. Half his paperwork was scattered all over the floor and there were tears in some of the rest.

He was amazed to find her that responsive after what she'd been through. She might have found her husband repulsive, but she was as helpless in Ted's arms now as she'd been the first time he'd ever kissed her. The knowledge of it, and the involuntary pride, filled his face as he watched her fumble under her floppy shirt with the catches to her brassiere.

She saw that expression and didn't understand it. Her hands finished closing the fastening and dropped to her sides. She stared at him, finding her own curiosity magnified in his eyes. He looked sexy, she thought, with his mouth faintly swollen from the long contact with hers, and his silver hair falling roguishly onto his forehead.

She searched for Shep, who'd given up on her and gone to sleep on the floor in the corner. "Some watchdog you are," she muttered at the sleeping puppy.

"I don't think he was convinced that you wanted to be rescued," Ted murmured.

She flushed, touching her shirt absently, wincing as her hand came into contact with the cut.

He scowled, understanding immediately. "I was too rough, wasn't I? I'm sorry. I realize that it must still be pretty sore."

"It's all right," she said. Her shy gaze dropped to his broad chest. "You didn't hurt me. There's something I'd like to ask you."

"Go ahead."

Her teeth nibbled at her lower lip. She could still taste him on it. "Is it only that good in the beginning?" She lifted her head, frowning worriedly as she met his curious eyes. "I mean, before people actually have se... when they get really intimate," she amended quickly.

Chapter Eight

He didn't look shocked, she thought. In fact, he was smiling. "No. It feels like that all the time, all the way," he said gently. "Especially when two people want each other so desperately."

"Oh." She squared her shoulders. "I've been lonely," she said abruptly, so that he wouldn't get the wrong idea about her headlong response.

It didn't work. He was looking more smug by the minute. "You *were* lonely," he echoed.

She glared at him. "Very lonely. I couldn't help it."

"Do I look as if I feel taken advantage of?" he asked pleasantly.

She searched for words and couldn't find any.

He leaned back against the desk, watching her. "You hated intimacy with Barry, didn't you?"

She hesitated. Then she nodded. "He said things..." She couldn't bear to remember them. "He hated the way I froze when he touched me. I couldn't bear for him to touch me. He liked to talk about what he did with other women—" She broke off and turned away. "Oh, God, you can't imagine what it was like!"

He moved behind her. His lean hands held her shoulders without pressure. "I'm getting a pretty raw picture of it," he said curtly. "But it's over now. You have to start putting it behind you."

She turned in his grasp, her blue eyes wide and frightened. "What if I can't? What if I really am cold, like he said?"

He pursed his lips and his eyes smiled at her. "Corrie," he said softly, "if I hadn't pulled back when I did, could you have stopped me?"

She felt the color whip up in her cheeks like a souf-flé.

"You're not cold," he assured her.

"But we didn't . . . !"

"If we had," he emphasized, "it wouldn't have been any different." His eyes held hers. She couldn't drag them away, and heat ran through her body like fire. "You might draw back at first, but it would only be a momentary withdrawal. I can make you so hungry that you could take me without preliminaries at all."

Her eyes showed the faint curiosity the remark brought forth.

"You don't understand? For a woman who was married, Corrie, you're singularly naive." He told her, bluntly, exactly what he meant, and her indrawn breath was audible.

"You don't know very much about your body, do you?" he asked quietly. "I'm sorry that you think sex is something dark and cruel. It isn't. It's a way of expressing feelings and needs that we can't put into words."

"Have you ever done it with someone you loved?" she asked, just as bluntly.

He hesitated. His chest rose and fell slowly. "No," he said after a minute. "I've enjoyed women and they've enjoyed me, on a no-strings basis. But I've been very careful about my liaisons. There's never been a commitment."

"And never will be," she said, echoing what he'd said before. "You've said so often enough."

His pale eyes narrowed as he studied her face. "You'll want to marry again," he said. "You're not the sort of woman who would feel comfortable having children without a husband."

She turned away, feeling empty as his hands left her shoulders. She wouldn't want children because they wouldn't be Ted's. How could she tell him that? "I don't want marriage or children anymore," she said dully.

"Coreen, all men aren't like Barry!"

She looked back at him solemnly. "How does a woman know before she marries a man what he'll be like as a husband? How does she know that he won't hurt her or abuse her, or be unfaithful to her?"

"If he loves her, that will all fall into place," he said curtly.

"Some men can't be tied down to just one woman," she replied. "You ought to know. You change your women like you change your saddles," she added ruefully. "Every other newspaper has you pictured with some new woman."

"Gossip pages run on gossip," he said shortly. "I enjoy the company of pretty women when I go out."

"Of course, and why shouldn't you? You're a bachelor. You have no ties, no responsibilities." She looked away from his curious expression. "But a married man should care enough to give up other women. Or at least, I used to think so. Barry never gave up anything."

"Barry didn't love you," he said flatly.

"He owned me," she replied. "He used to say that he bought and paid for me, and maybe he did. God knows, Dad would never have been so comfortable at the end if he hadn't intervened. And I'd have had no place at all to go."

Ted didn't like remembering that. He'd given her no help, offered no comfort. Even if he'd wanted to, Barry made sure that he kept the two of them separated. He was jealous, Ted realized now. Barry had noticed the looks Ted was giving Coreen and it had made him want her, but only to keep her from Ted. Why hadn't he ever realized that Barry competed with him? Barry had lied to both of them, to keep them apart. And he hadn't known.

Coreen noticed Ted's angry scowl and turned away. "Sorry," she said. "I don't mean to keep dragging the past up."

"Yes, I know." His eyes were faintly sad as they searched over her. "I'm sorry that we can't change it."

She shrugged. "Everyone goes through unpleasantness. We just have to remember that there's always a light at the end of the tunnel."

"Is there?" He held her eyes with his. "You're vulnerable with me. Is it because Barry was cruel to you, or is it because we never made love and you're curious?"

She lifted her chin. "Maybe it's both."

"Maybe it's neither." He stuck his hands into his pockets and studied her mutinous face. "But the years are still wrong. You need a young man."

"So you keep saying. If you believe it, why did you send Barney away?"

He glared at her. "Don't you have something to do?"

She sighed. "I wish I did. Sandy once said you needed help in here. I can type. And I can take dictation, if you don't go too fast."

He glanced at the desk irritably, noticing its disorder and remembering how it came to be in such a mess.

"You can start with that," he said, nodding his head toward it. "And next time I lay you down, I won't stop," he added unexpectedly.

She lifted both eyebrows in what she hoped was sophisticated cynicism. "If you don't, you'll marry me," she said with equal candor.

Once, the very word marriage would have stopped him in his tracks. Now, he didn't find it so threatening. And the more he was around Coreen, the hungrier and lonelier he felt. He glared at her.

"I'd better practice more control, in that case," he said mockingly.

"Yes, perhaps you should." She wasn't going to back down ever again, she decided. Her eyes met his bravely. "I'm not taking anything these days."

His cheeks went ruddy and she noticed that his eyes began to darken as they fell suddenly, explicitly, to her waistline.

"You're too old for children, remember?" she said with pure sarcasm.

He looked back up. His eyebrows arched. "I'm not too old to make them," he said with a soft threat in his deep voice. "So don't push too hard."

She felt alive; more alive than she had since she was single and Ted had been her whole world. She didn't understand her own bravado. But she did know that she wasn't afraid of what he was threatening. She wasn't afraid of him at all.

"If we had a child," she said deliberately, "it would have blue eyes."

His jaw tautened. He didn't reply. He turned away from her to look for his hat. "I have some business to take care of. If you want to tidy the office, go ahead. But don't move anything off the desk. I'll never be able to find it again."

"Okay."

"Where's Shep?"

"Over there." She gestured at the corner, and grinned. "Mrs. Bird boiled him a drumstick but he left it, to follow me."

He smiled at her. "You and that pup."

"He's the most wonderful present I ever had. I mean it."

"I know." He paused beside her on his way out and tilted her face up to his with a tender hand so that he could search her eyes. "I like seeing you smile. You don't do it very often these days."

"I'm getting better."

He nodded. His gaze fell to her mouth and the fingers on her chin went rigid.

"Afraid to kiss me?" she whispered boldly.

He smiled faintly. "Maybe I am. You and I are explosive."

Her eyes were curious. "Isn't it always like that, for a man?"

His thumb slid over her chin and moved up to tug at her soft lower lip. "Not for me," he confessed quietly. "I only feel this fever with you, Corrie," he whispered against her mouth as he took it.

It was a mistake. He knew it the minute he felt her lips part beneath the ardent pressure of his mouth. He groaned and dropped his hat on the floor in the rush of his need to get her against him. He half lifted her into his aroused body and his tongue penetrated the soft depths of her mouth. He felt her shiver and heard her moan, and the world spun away.

Someone was knocking at the door. He heard it, as if from deep in a well. He lifted his head and found himself fighting to breathe. Coreen's eyes were half-closed with desire, her mouth swollen and red, her body arched slightly, yielded, waiting. His hand was smoothing hungrily over her undamaged breast and he felt her heart beating like mad under it.

"What is it?" His voice sounded hoarse, even when he raised it.

"That man's here about the new combine, Mr. Regan!" one of his men called through the door.

"Tell him I'll be there in ten minutes!" he yelled back.

"Yes, sir!"

Footsteps died away. Coreen hadn't moved, or protested, or tried to pull away.

"Do you want more?" he asked coolly, angered by his own weakness.

She had no pride left. "Yes," she whispered, "please."

"Corrie...!"

"Please," she whispered again, tugging at his head.

Her eyes closed as he bent helplessly to her waiting mouth. The kiss was deeper this time, slower, more achingly thorough than ever before. His powerful legs trembled as she pushed closer to his aroused body and he felt her softness and warmth against him.

His lean hands found her hips and tugged her rhythmically against him while he kissed her until he had to stop for air.

"Do you realize that I could take you right here, standing up, right now?" he asked in a rough whisper.

"Yes," she said simply.

He parted her lips with his, and pushed his tongue slowly past her teeth once, twice, deeper with each movement. "Open your mouth a little more," he whispered raggedly. "Let me touch you...more deeply... inside!"

She cried out at the imagery and her whole body vibrated as he deepened the kiss to blatant intimacy. His legs parted and he pulled her between them, raising her so that they were perfectly matched, male to female. He groaned so harshly that her nails bit into him as she tried to get even closer, to satisfy the hunger in him that she could almost taste.

Her fingers went, trembling in their haste, to the buttons on his shirt. He made a feeble attempt to stay them, knowing too well what was going to happen to him if she touched his chest. But he didn't really want to stop her. Seconds later, when he felt her fingers caressing through the thick mat of hair that covered him to the waist and below, he shuddered and cried out.

She caught her breath at the unfamiliar sound. It excited her even more to know that she could arouse him so easily. Instinctively, her mouth moved down to his chest and pressed hungrily against it through the thick mat of hair. His heartbeat shook her for the one, long instant that he gave in to his own need.

"No," he ground out, shuddering as he finally managed to pull her away and hold her back from him with bruising hands while there was still time. "Oh, God...no, Corrie!" he said hoarsely.

She lifted her face and looked into his ravaged eyes with slowly dawning comprehension. "I'd let you," she whispered feverishly.

His eyes closed and his teeth ground together. His hands on her shoulders hurt her while he fought his own desperate need.

"Ted, I'd let you," she repeated brokenly.

He rested his damp forehead against hers and dragged in enough breath to fill his lungs. "No. I could make you pregnant," he whispered, shaken.

He sounded as if that would be the end of the world as far as he was concerned. He didn't want a child. He didn't want commitment. In the fever of their kisses, she'd forgotten. But he hadn't. He was shaken, but not enough to forget the possible consequences of making love to her.

She took a long, shaky breath. "Yes," she said a minute later, "that's right. Silly of me...not to remember."

He barely heard her. His body was in the grip of a kind of pain he hadn't experienced since adolescence.

"Stand still, honey," he whispered roughly. "Don't make it worse...."

She hadn't realized that she was shifting restlessly, brushing his hard body. She stood very still while he concentrated on his breathing until the rigor of his body began to relax. She watched him unashamedly, learning things about him, about men, that she hadn't known. Her eyes were curious, running over him like hands, searching out all the signs that gave away his raging desire and its slow—very slow—containment.

He felt her rapt eyes on his face. "Stop staring," he muttered as he took one last breath and the steely fingers on her shoulders began to relax.

"I'm curious," she said simply, and her gaze was faintly self-conscious. "I've never seen you like this."

His eyes speared into hers. "Proud of yourself?" he asked curtly.

She nodded. "In a way. Nobody ever wanted me that much. Does it hurt?"

He laughed coldly. "My God...!"

"Well, does it?" she persisted. "Some books say it does and some say it doesn't, but they all agree that a man can control it if he has to. Barry said he couldn't, and that was why he hurt me. But it wasn't true, was it?"

He let out one last deep breath. "It depends on how aroused he is." His eyes narrowed. "Did you work him up the way you just worked me up, and then refuse him?"

The light went out of her. He couldn't seem to accept that it wasn't her fault. She didn't realize that it was frustration talking.

She moved back from him. "I couldn't have worked him up if I'd been a born seductress," she said with quiet pride. "He pretended that I was cold. The fact was, he didn't want me. He never wanted me, not physically. He was…" She couldn't say it. She couldn't get the word out.

He was still straining to breathe normally. "He was what?"

"It doesn't really matter, does it? He's dead." She went to the office door and opened it. "I'd like a cup of coffee. I'll start working in here after I've had it, if that's all right."

"I'll be gone in five minutes," he said flatly. "You can start when I leave."

She nodded. She didn't look back on her way to the kitchen.

Ted went out the door in a flaming rage. Twice in one day he'd let her knock his legs out from under him. She'd seen how vulnerable he was to her, and put a weapon in her hands that she could break him with if she chose. He'd never been so helpless. Did she know? Of course she knew! And she had every reason in the world to use his own weakness against him. He didn't know how he was going to protect himself.

He couldn't come straight back home, he knew that. What he needed was breathing space. That was it. He needed a business trip. He walked toward the waiting mechanic down by the garage where the combine sat, racking his brain all the way for a legitimate reason to leave the ranch.

* * *

Coreen sat down to supper with Sandy, who seemed unusually quiet and puzzled. They started without Ted, and Mrs. Bird had only set two places.

"Is something wrong?" Coreen asked Sandy.

"I don't know." She studied the younger woman with evident puzzlement. "Have you and Ted had an argument?"

Coreen quickly lowered her eyes. "Sort of," she said. "Why?"

"He phoned Mrs. Bird and said that he was going to Nassau this afternoon. Without coming home to change, without packing..."

Coreen felt the blow all the way to her knees. So his opinion of her was really that low, was it? Now he thought she'd be laying in wait for him, trying to seduce him into marriage. He already thought she'd teased Barry into suicide by denying him her body. God knew what he thought of her after this afternoon's episode.

"I see," she said when she realized that Sandy was waiting for an answer.

"And he took Lillian with him, apparently."

That was the final straw. Coreen put down her fork and burst into tears.

"That's what I thought," Sandy murmured sadly. She got up and took Coreen into her arms. "Poor baby," she sympathized soothingly. "Love doesn't die just because we want it to, does it? Even after the way he's treated you, you can't stop."

"I hate him!" She choked. "I hate him!"

"Of course you do," Sandy said, comforting her. "He's an animal."

"He thinks I drove Barry to suicide by teasing him." She whimpered. "He still thinks I killed him!"

"No, he doesn't. He's just fighting a rear-guard action. He's convinced himself that he's too old for you and he isn't going to give in. He's let our childhood warp his whole life. I'm sorry that he's hurting you like this."

Coreen cried until her throat was raw. Then she dabbed at her eyes with the hem of her blouse and took the tissue Sandy handed her and blew her nose.

"I can't stay here anymore," she told Sandy when she was calm. "It's tearing me apart."

"I know. But you're not strong enough."

"I am. If you'll let me rent the apartment, and Ted will give me the living allowance he promised, I think I'm well enough to get a job. I can type and I can take dictation. There must be somebody in Victoria who'll hire me."

Sandy grimaced. "This won't do," she said. "You can't..."

"I have to!" Coreen's eyes were tortured. "I'd go to him on my knees, begging for anything he cared to give me, if I stayed. Don't you see? I love him!"

Sandy ground her teeth. "That bad, huh?"

"Oh, yes." Coreen laughed bitterly. "That bad. And he doesn't want commitment, children, or me in that order. He said so before he left." She didn't mention what had prompted it, or the close call they'd had in Ted's study.

She didn't need to. Sandy's eyes were shrewd and she wasn't blind to the tension between her best friend and her brother.

"He'll kill me when he comes back and finds you gone," she told Coreen.

"No, he won't. He'll be relieved," came the weary reply. "Will you help me?"

Sandy sighed heavily. "I don't suppose I have a choice."

Coreen smiled. "No. Neither do I. I'll be fine," she added reassuringly. "I'm much better."

Sandy didn't argue. Heaven knew, it was going to be unbearable for Coreen if Ted was as determined as usual to keep her at arm's length. The evidence of two years ago was still disturbing.

"What about Shep?" she asked.

Coreen didn't like thinking about leaving her puppy. "He'll have to stay here," she said miserably.

"I'll bring him to visit on weekends, how about that?" Sandy asked.

Coreen smiled through her tears. "You're the best friend I have."

"And you're mine. I wish my brother was less of a trial to both of us!"

A wish that Coreen silently affirmed.

Two days later, packed and silent, she rode to Victoria ahead of Sandy with her bags in the small foreign car that Sandy had loaned her to drive. Her ribs were still a little sore, but she was more than capable of getting around by herself.

The apartment was spacious, big enough for two people to share and not run into each other. It even had a nice view. The girls stocked the refrigerator and shelves and then it was time for Sandy to go.

"You know the number at the ranch if you need me," she told Coreen, "and I'll be up with Shep next Saturday. You're sure you'll be all right?"

"This is Victoria, not New York," she murmured with a smile. "I'm perfectly safe here."

"I do hope so. Mrs. Lowery and her husband live in the unit next door. They're sweet old people. If you get in trouble, all you have to do is knock on the door. Mr. Lowery is a retired police officer," she added with a grin.

"I'll remember. Thanks, Sandy. For everything."

Sandy glowered at her. "I should have done this sooner," she said. "I kept hoping that Ted might relent. I should have known better. He's too old to change his ways now."

"That isn't really surprising, is it?" Coreen asked sadly. "If he'd wanted to marry anyone, he'd have done it long before now. I've been living in dreams. I always thought that if you loved somebody enough, they'd have to love you back. But it isn't like that." She brushed back her thick, short hair. "Amazing, isn't it, that I'm still mooning over the same man? And he still doesn't want me."

"I think you're wrong about that," Sandy said quietly. "I think he wants you very much."

"But not for keeps" came the sad reply.

Sandy couldn't deny it. Ted had made his choice very apparent. He was willing to leave the country with one woman to make another woman leave him alone. He gave hard lessons. Coreen wouldn't forget this one very soon.

"I'll see you Saturday. Call if you need anything."

Coreen assured her that she would. When the door closed, she was truly alone for the first time in years. Once she got used to it, she told herself, she was probably going to enjoy it. It was getting used to it that was going to be hard.

She spent a lonely weekend, hoping all the time that the telephone would ring and Ted would tell her he'd made a terrible mistake. She listened for his knock at the door. But Monday came, and Ted didn't. He was in Nassau with Lillian. Presumably he'd been making his feelings clear to Coreen. And he had. This time, she got the message. By Monday, she was resigned to a future that wouldn't ever contain Ted.

Sandy had given her a couple of places to apply for work, and she went not only to those, but to four others that she found on the bulletin board in the labor office. And miracle of miracles, one of her job leads panned out the very same day. A local real estate office had an immediate opening for a receptionist, and Coreen was exactly what the woman who ran the office had in mind.

She started work Tuesday. Her typing speed suited the agency very well, and her personality proved an asset to the business. She fielded appointments for her boss and the other four agents who worked out of the small office as if she'd been born to it. She went home tired at the end of the long day, because she wasn't used to this sort of work, but she loved what she was doing and it showed. She felt safe, secure in her own ability to hold down a job and pay the rent. Her self-esteem blossomed.

By Saturday, when Sandy arrived with an excited Shep in the car with her, Coreen was beaming. She'd had her hair trimmed and was wearing new clothes. She looked bright and happy, and the dark shadows under her blue eyes were beginning to recede.

"You look so much better!" Sandy exclaimed. "I can't get over the change in you!"

"Isn't it great?" came the bubbling reply. "I never dreamed how much fun it would be to work like this, with only myself to provide for. I make a salary with my own two hands and I don't have to ask anybody for anything! I won't even need the allowance from the trust, and I can pay rent on the apartment, too!"

Sandy looked hesitant. "Don't get too independent too soon, will you? Take it easy. You're still not completely well, and you could overextend yourself."

"Don't be such a worrywort," Coreen teased. By this time, she was on the floor playing with Shep. "He's grown, hasn't he? Oh, I miss him so!"

She missed Ted, too, and watching the trainer work out with the horses. But she had to put up a good front. She couldn't let them think that she was pining for the ranch. For him.

It was such a good front that she convinced Sandy entirely. The older woman went back home morose and quiet, so that Mrs. Bird walked around worrying for another week.

Ted came home two weeks after he'd left, and in between there hadn't been a telephone call or even a postcard. He looked haggard. His tan was the only healthy-looking thing about him. His temper certainly hadn't improved in his absence. He was out near the stable giving two of his men hell over some tasks he'd assigned that hadn't gotten finished by his return.

He stormed back in just in time for supper. He sat down at the table and frowned when he noticed that Mrs. Bird had only set two places.

Sandy helped herself to roast and mashed potatoes while Ted fought not to ask the question he dreaded putting into words.

"Don't bother looking for her," Sandy said after a minute. "She's gone."

Chapter Nine

"Coreen's gone?" Ted echoed. He glowered at his sister. "Where has she gone?"

"She moved up to Victoria two weeks ago. I've let her rent the apartment there. She has a job, too. She's receptionist to a real estate agency, and she's blooming."

It took him a minute to adjust to the news. He hadn't expected her to leave. He'd stayed away, hoping to get his passion for her under control before it broke the bonds completely. The way they'd loved had been so sweet that he hadn't slept a night since. He wanted her to the point of madness, but he couldn't afford to give in. It was what was best for her, he'd told himself when he left. But two weeks of self-denial had only made him bad-tempered. All he could think about was the years of anguish she'd spent with Barry because of him. He'd wanted to spare her the ordeal of being tied to an older man and being discontent. But he'd caused her such pain, all from noble motives. And what he'd done to himself didn't bear thinking about.

Then he remembered without wanting to that he'd found a job for Barney in Victoria. Did Coreen know that was where Barney was? Was that why she'd wanted to go there? She must have thought about why Ted had left so abruptly, and put his absence down to revulsion at her abandon in his arms or fear of being seduced by her. He'd even taunted her with Barry in his fervor to keep her from seeing his weakness for her. Had his abrupt departure pushed her into another man's arms, for the second time?

"Oh, no," he said wearily. He rested his forehead on his raised fists, propped on the table by his elbows. "God, not again!"

"What are you groaning about? By the way, how's Lillian?" Sandy asked pointedly while she munched on a small piece of roast beef.

"I don't know."

"You took her to Nassau. Did you misplace her?" she taunted.

He lifted his head and glared at her. "She was on the same plane with me. We weren't together."

"You said you were. You told Mrs. Bird you were."

He groaned again.

"It's just as well. Coreen cried for two days before she went to Victoria," she said, putting the knife into his heart with venomous accuracy. She wasn't sorry when he went pale. "She left here cursing you for all she was worth. But when I saw her Saturday, she was as bright as a sunbeam. She didn't even mention you."

He glared at his sister.

She ate another piece of meat. "This is delicious. Lost your appetite?" she asked pleasantly.

He pushed the plate aside and drank his coffee black. "Yes."

"You said that you didn't want her often enough. She finally listened. Aren't you glad?" she added.

He didn't answer her. He drank some more coffee.

"You're too old for her, remember?" she persisted. "And you don't want children. She's still young. She wants to get married and have a family. I heard Barney say the same thing to his father last month, that he was ready to settle down." She brightened as Ted went pale. "Say, didn't you get him a job in Victoria? Won't it be funny if they meet up there and end up married?"

Ted got up from the table, so sick that he couldn't look at food. He walked blindly into his study and slammed the door viciously behind him. He walked to the portable bar and picked up the whiskey bottle.

"No," he told himself. "No, this isn't the answer."

He stared at the squat crystal decanter and at the glass. "On second thought," he muttered, pulling out the stopper, "why the hell not?"

He was well into his second glass when he sat down behind the desk and let his imagination run wild. Coreen had probably already found Barney or vice versa. They were probably out together tonight, at a movie or a theater. He might even have driven her up to Houston to a show. He glowered at the desk, remembering how it had felt to have her lying on her back under his aching body, giving him kiss for feverish kiss. Would she kiss Barney that way?

He doggedly refused to remember that it hadn't been Coreen who'd pulled back at all. It had been himself. She'd even offered...

"No!"

His own voice shocked him. He was letting this business go to his head. His hormones were manipulating him. He couldn't give in, now. He knew that he was wrong for Coreen. She was too young for him. Even if she'd told the truth and she hadn't been able to want Barry, maybe she'd only turned to Ted out of frustration. After all, she'd wanted him years ago and he'd pushed her away. Maybe it was curiosity.

His clouded mind raced on. Or was it that she'd just rediscovered her femininity? She'd discovered that she could want someone after all, and he was male and handy. He didn't like that thought at all. He'd come home convinced that he was never going to be cured of his passion for her. He wanted her. He needed her. His own principles weren't enough to save him from his hunger. If she'd been here when he got home, nothing would have spared her. But she was gone, and he was caught between his hunger and his conscience all over again.

Despite her bad marriage, she was still capable of passion. Would it be the same with Barney that it had been with him? If it was only desire, wouldn't she be able to feel it for someone else as well as himself? Barry had treated her badly, but she'd wanted Ted so much. His head spun remembering how much. She'd begged him...

He took another drink, trying to drown out the sight of her drowsy, soft eyes as she begged for his mouth. He couldn't bear to remember that he'd pushed her away so cruelly and left. He always left, but she went with him anyway. That didn't make sense. But then, not much did. He stared at the decanter. How many drinks had he had: one or two? Or was it three? He was beginning to lose count. He was also feeling better about the situation. If only he could remember what the situation was. . . .

Sandy found him slumped over the desk an hour later. She clucked her tongue.

"Poor old thing," she murmured, moving the whiskey decanter back to the bar. "You just won't give an inch, will you?"

"She left me," he drawled half-consciously.

"You left her," she corrected him. "She's in love with you."

"No," he replied. "She never loved me. Too young to love like that."

"Love doesn't have an age limit," she told him. "She loved you all those long years, and you never did anything but push her away. First it was Barry. Now it's going to be Barney. She'll ruin her life. She'll waste it with other men, when all she wants in the world is just you, gray hair and all."

"Oh, God, I'm too old!" he growled. "Too old to be her husband, to be a father! She'd get tired of me, don't you see? She'd want someone younger, and I wouldn't be able to let her go!"

She frowned and stopped in place, staring down at him incredulously. Did he realize what he was admitting?

"Ted?" she said softly.

He put his head in his hands. "Nobody else," he said dizzily. "Nobody, since the first time I saw her, standing in the feed store in that old blouse and shorts. Wanted her so much. Wanted her more...than my own life. Never anybody else, in my life, in my heart, in my bed..." He sighed heavily and slumped, his head on his forearms. Beside him, Sandy gaped at his still figure. Why...he loved Coreen!

She didn't know what to do. She couldn't betray him. On the other hand, was he going to ruin his life and Coreen's by keeping his feelings to himself? She had to do something. But what!

In the end, there was nothing she could do. She half led, half carried him to the sofa and dumped him there, with a quilt from his bed for cover.

"You're going to hate yourself," she told his unconscious figure.

It was much later before he came out of it, groaning and holding his head. He was violently ill and he had a headache that wouldn't quit. He went to bed, oblivious to Sandy's worried eyes following him, and didn't surface until the next day.

By then, he was himself again, rigidly controlled and giving away nothing at all. He sat down to breakfast looking as bright as a new penny. Without a word, he dared Sandy to mention the day before.

"I have a job in Victoria today," she informed him. "I may stay overnight with Coreen, if I'm very late."

"Suit yourself."

She didn't look up. "Any messages?"

His pale eyes met hers head-on. "No."

She leaned back in her chair with her second cup of coffee in her hand. "You've already wasted two years of your life, and hers, being noble," she said bluntly. "Barney is just like Barry, happy-go-lucky and as shallow as a fish pond. He probably wouldn't hurt her, but she'd be just as unhappy with him. Suppose she falls headlong into another bad marriage?"

He didn't react at all. "It's her life. She has to make her own mistakes."

"You're her biggest one," she said, irritated beyond discretion. She put the cup down hard. "She's never loved anyone else. I don't think she can. And she's had nothing from you except rejection and heartache and cruelty." She got up from the table, glaring at him. "I'm sorry I ever became friends with her. Maybe if I hadn't, she'd have been spared all this misery."

His pale eyes lanced into hers. "You have no right to pry into my private life. Or Coreen's."

"I'm not trying to," she returned. "I won't make any attempts to play Cupid, I promise you. In return, you might consider keeping a respectful distance while Coreen gets over the last few miserable years of her life."

He glanced down at his plate. "That's what I intended all along."

"Good. Maybe I'm wrong about Barney. Maybe he'll be the best thing that ever happened to her."

His hand clenched on his coffee cup. "Maybe he will."

She hesitated, but there was really nothing more to say. She left him sitting there, his eyes downcast and unreadable.

Coreen had, indeed, discovered Barney. Rather, he'd discovered her, at a local fast-food joint one day when they were both catching a quick bite to eat. She'd been delighted to find a familiar face, and he was already infatuated with her. It had been a short jump from there to one date, and then another.

Sandy had come up for the night while she was on a job, and she hadn't mentioned Ted at all. But Coreen had mentioned Barney. She was enjoying her life, having decided that loving Ted was going to kill her if she didn't put a stop to it.

She put on a good front. Sandy could see right through it, and she hated the pain she read in Coreen's blue eyes when she didn't think it was showing. She hoped Ted knew what he was doing. He might have just lost his last chance for happiness. But she wished Coreen well, all the same. If Barney could make her happy—well, she deserved some happiness.

But love didn't develop between the two of them. Coreen enjoyed Barney's company, and he hers. They both knew that friendship was all they could expect, and not only because of Coreen's lingering feeling for Ted. Barney had found a woman whom he adored, too, but she was married. There was no hope at the moment that anything could develop there. He was like Coreen: awash in a tempest of feelings that he could never express.

It gave them something in common, and bound them closer together. Since they enjoyed the same sort of movies, they started sharing rental costs and spending Friday evenings at the apartment, watching the latest releases over popcorn and soft drinks.

When Sandy discovered this new ritual, she was amused at the innocence of it. Occasionally she dropped in to share the popcorn, and she and Barney became friends, too.

"You're spending a lot of time in Victoria lately," Ted said one Friday afternoon. "What's the attraction?"

"I like to see Coreen. And Barney, of course."

He went very still. "Barney?"

"I go up occasionally to watch movies with them at the apartment on Friday nights," she explained innocently. "They're always together these days. Friday is movie night."

His eyes flashed. "They're sleeping together in my apartment?" he blurted out furiously.

"Do you realize what you're saying?" she asked quietly. "Think, Ted. Is that really the sort of woman you think Coreen is?"

He was insanely jealous. He couldn't begin to think through his violent emotions. Coreen, with Barney...

"Don't you even realize how cruel Barry was to her?" she persisted. "Do you seriously believe that she could lead some sort of promiscuous existence after what she suffered with him? Don't you know that she's frightened of intimacy?"

"Not with me, she isn't," he said bluntly, and before he thought.

Her eyes widened and her mouth snapped shut.

"I haven't seduced her, if that's what the disapproving look signifies," he said with a mocking smile. "I still have a few principles that I haven't sold-out."

"You might have spared her that," she said.

"She might have spared me as well," he returned.

She relented a little. "I'm sorry. I suppose you think you're doing it for her, don't you?"

He averted his face. "You remember how it was when we were kids."

"And you don't," she said curtly. "Mother didn't love him. She never loved him. She loved what he had. She didn't even want us, because we interfered with her life-style. But he insisted, because he was crazy about kids."

"She loved him when they got married," he said doggedly.

"You don't believe that. You haven't believed it for a long time. It's something you've held on to, to give you a reason to keep Coreen at arm's length."

He didn't answer her. She could see the indecision and the pain in his face.

"Spill it," she said abruptly. "Come on, let's have all of it. What's the real reason?"

It was a shot in the dark, but his face went pale. So there was something...!

"Tell me!" she demanded.

He ground his teeth together. "Barry said that what she loved was my money. When I wouldn't play ball, she settled for his."

"And you believed him."

"It made sense. Look at me," he muttered. "I'm sixteen years her senior. Barry said we looked ridiculous together, that people laughed at the age difference."

"Barry was jealous of you, and he played on your conscience," Sandy replied. "You don't really believe these things, Ted. You can't."

He pushed the coffee cup away from his restless fingers and leaned back. "It happened once before," he reminded her. "When I was twenty-six, and I thought I might marry Edie."

"And then discovered that she was already bragging to her friends about all the expensive things she was going to buy herself when she got you to the altar. I remember."

He smiled faintly. "So do I," he said. "Coreen wants me, all right. She always has. But wanting isn't enough. And right now, I can't be sure that she isn't trying to gain back the self-esteem she lost because Barry called her frigid."

"Maybe she is," she said. "If that's the case, it's Barney who's helping her get it back."

His face went hard. "He's closer to her own age."

"Yes, he is," she agreed pleasantly. "And they get on like a house on fire. He treats her so gently. Nothing like Barry did. He takes her out and buys her flowers and even cooks supper for her when she's tired. Quite a guy, Barney."

He felt, and looked, sick to his stomach. He hadn't thought it was serious. From the tidbits of gossip Sandy let slip, he'd convinced himself that as far as Coreen was concerned, Barney was more like a girlfriend with chest hair than a boyfriend. Now, he wasn't so sure.

"I see."

"I'm glad you've decided to let go, Ted," she said gently. "It's a kindness, if you have nothing to give her. She's finding her own way now, standing on her own feet for the first time in her life. Away from you, she's a different woman."

"Different how?" he asked.

"She's happy," she said.

He got up from the table and left the room without another word. Watching him go, Sandy regretted what she'd said. If Coreen was just putting on an act, if she

did still love Ted, then what Sandy had just told him
might have destroyed her last chance for happiness.

It was Sunday. Coreen had gone to church with Barney and seen him off on a two-day business trip at the
Victoria airport afterward. The apartment was very
quiet now, and she couldn't find anything on television
that she really wanted to watch.

The buzz of the doorbell was almost welcome, except that it was probably going to be a salesman or a
neighbor wanting to chat. She wasn't in the mood for
either.

Jeaned and T-shirted, and barefoot, she went to the
door muttering and peeped through the keyhole. Her
hand froze on the chain latch. She stared, drinking in
the angry face of the man she'd hoped she might forget. Her eyes closed and she leaned against the door
with her heart pounding audibly in her chest. *Ted!* It
was Ted, and she loved him and wanted him. And he
wanted no part of her.

"Open the door, Coreen," he said shortly.

"How do you know I'm home?" she demanded angrily. "I might be out, for all you know!"

"Obviously you aren't."

She sighed. If she'd kept her big mouth shut...

She pulled aside the chain latch and unwillingly
opened the door. "Come in," she said in a subdued
tone. "It's your apartment after all. I'm just the ten-
ant."

He paused to close the door behind him before he
followed her into the living room and sailed his cream-
colored Stetson onto the counter of the bar. He was
dressed in a suit and tie and he looked formal. His eyes

drifted down to her pretty bare feet and he concealed a smile. Her slender figure was very well outlined in the close-fitting jeans she had on, and the T-shirt was almost see-through, despite its colorful message that invited people to visit Texas.

"How are you?" he asked.

She sat down on the arm of the big armchair. "As you see."

His pale eyes went around the room. There was no sign of occupation. She was here, but she'd made no mark on the room at all.

"I haven't trashed the furniture," she said, misunderstanding his scrutiny.

"No wrestling matches with Barney on my sofa on Friday nights?" he chided with more venom than he knew.

She lifted her chin. "We can always watch movies at Barney's apartment if you don't like me bringing him here," she said.

His eyes flashed angrily. They pinned her, making her feel like backing away. But she didn't. She'd gained new self-confidence over the weeks since Barry's death— mainly because of Ted himself. She stood her ground, and admiration filtered through the anger in his eyes.

"I don't give a damn what you do with Barney," he said.

As if she didn't already know that. His absence from her life in recent weeks had made his lack of interest plain.

But he looked worn. There was no other word to describe it. His lean face had deep hollows in it, and there were new lines around his firm mouth and between his eyes.

"You look tired," she said with involuntary gentleness.

Her words hardened him visibly, and at once.

"Oh, I know," she said heavily, "you don't want concern from me. God forbid that I should worry about you."

He stuck his hands into the pockets of his expensive slacks and went to stand by the window. It was a hazy summer day. He watched the clouds shift on the horizon, dark and threatening clouds that carried the promise of rain.

"Why did you come, Ted?" she asked after the long silence grew tedious.

He didn't turn. "I wanted to make sure that you were all right."

She didn't read anything into that statement. She stared at his back without blinking. "I'm fine. I have a good job and I'm making friends. I'll be able to do without that allowance, in fact. If I refuse it, can you give it to charity?"

He turned, frowning. "There's no need for gestures," he said coldly.

"It isn't a gesture. I don't want Barry's money. I never did." She smiled at his expression. "Disappointed? I know you'd rather think that I married him for all that nice money."

He didn't react at all. "There's no provision if you refuse the money. The trust will remain untouched."

She shrugged. "Then do what you like about it. But I won't accept it. I wouldn't have married Barry if it hadn't been for Papa, anyway. At least one good thing came out of it—he had the medical care he needed."

"Why didn't you ask me for help?" he demanded.

She lifted both eyebrows, astonished. "It never would have occurred to me," she stammered.

"Your father was a friend of mine, as well as a business acquaintance," he said curtly. "I would have done anything I could for him."

She averted her eyes.

He moved closer. Something about her posture disturbed him. "You're hiding something."

She hesitated, but he looked capable of standing there all night until he got an answer. "Barry warned me not to ask you for any financial help. He said that you'd told him you wanted me to marry him and get out of your hair. He made sure that I knew not to ask you."

His breath left in a violent rush. "My God," he said roughly. "So that was it."

"I didn't really need telling, Ted," she added quietly. "You'd made it clear that you wanted nothing to do with me. Even when Dad was so sick, you hardly came near the place. And when you did..."

"When I did, I had nothing kind to say to you," he finished for her. "Barry kept me upset. He wouldn't let me near you, did you know that? He said that you hated me."

Her eyes lifted to his in time to see the flash of pain those memories kindled in his face.

"But I told him no such thing," she said hesitantly.

"Didn't you?" He laughed bitterly. "He said that you'd agreed to marry him because you thought he had more money than I did."

Chapter Ten

Coreen just stared at him. She wasn't going to make any more denials. If he believed her mercenary, let him.

He smiled at her stony countenance. "Yes, I know," he murmured, "I always think the worst of you, don't I? But he made it all sound so logical. Lie after lie, for two years and more, and I swallowed every one."

She traced a tiny smear of oil on the knee of her jeans. "They weren't all lies," she said. "He told you I was frigid, and I am."

"Not with me."

She lifted her eyes to his face. "There's more to intimacy than a few kisses, and you know it. You know what I mean, too. I destroyed him in bed. I made him incapable, every time..."

His face fascinated her. It looked like an image frozen in ice. "Do you realize what you're telling me?" he asked slowly.

"Yes," she said stiffly. "I'm telling you that I wasn't woman enough..."

"No!" He knelt beside the armchair, his eyes so close to hers that they filled the world. "Did he ever make love to you completely?"

"Completely?"

He told her, explicitly.

"Ted, for God's sake...!" She exploded.

She got up, and so did he. He caught her arms before she could move away. His face was drawn, almost white. He shook her gently. "Tell me!" he demanded.

"All right! No, he...he didn't!"

He didn't react for several seconds. When he did, it changed him. All the color rushed back into his lean face. He looked at Coreen with wonder, with fascination.

"You're still a virgin," he said unsteadily.

She glared at him. "Rub it in."

He couldn't seem to accept what he'd heard. He bit off a curse and got up, moving away from her. It had been bad enough before. Now it was unbearable. Corrie had never had a man. She'd been married, abused, tormented, but she'd never been intimate with Barry. She was chaste, in every real respect.

He ran his hand over his forehead, feeling perspiration there despite the air-conditioning in the apartment.

"What difference does it make now?" she asked angrily. "He's dead!"

"You really don't know, do you?" he asked. He didn't look at her.

"Know what?"

His hands balled into fists in his pockets. His head was bowed while he fought needs and desires that almost exploded into action.

He took a long breath and stared out the window. "How do you feel about Barney?" He glanced over his shoulder at her. "And please don't, for God's sake, tell me it's none of my business."

"It isn't," she said doggedly. But she relented. "He's my friend. We enjoy the same things."

"Do you love him?"

Her eyes answered him long before she averted them. "I like him," she hedged. "I'm not ready to love anyone," she added firmly. "I've just come through a disastrous marriage."

"I know that." He let out a long breath and turned to look at her, perched on the arm of the chair, looking belligerent and pretty. "Are you happy, Corrie?"

"Who is?" she replied quietly, with a cynicism far beyond her years. She tucked a lock of hair behind one small ear. "I'm content."

"Content." What a lukewarm word. It didn't suit someone like Corrie, who had been bright and beautiful before Barry made a hell of her life. Truthfully he hadn't done much to make her happy himself. All these years, he'd been thinking about himself, about protecting his heart from being broken, about preventing Corrie from taking over his life. He hadn't given a thought to how badly he was hurting her with his indifference, his cruelty.

"There must have been times when you blamed me for a lot of your problems," he said.

"Don't flatter yourself. I can make my own mistakes and pay for them. I don't have to blame them on other people."

He traced a pattern on the bar next to him. "I used to think that I didn't, either." His eyes were faraway, wistful. "Perhaps our view of ourselves is corrupted."

"You don't need anyone." She laughed. "You're completely self-sufficient."

His head turned toward her. "All I have is Sandy," he said quietly. "No one else. When she marries, I'll be completely alone with my principles and my conscience and my noble ideals. Do you think they'll keep me warm on long winter nights, Corrie, when I'm hungry for a woman in my arms in the darkness?"

She didn't like that thought. "You don't have any trouble getting women."

He lifted an eyebrow. "Getting them, no. I'm sinfully rich."

"Everyone knows that."

He nodded. "That's the problem. At my age, I never know the real motive when women come on to me."

It sounded as if he might be trying to tell her something. She didn't know what. A brief silence fell between them. "Would you like some coffee?" she asked finally.

He nodded.

She went into the kitchen to make it, aware at intervals of his studious gaze from the living room. But he didn't join her, not until she had everything on a tray. He met her at the kitchen door and carried the tray to the coffee table.

"I made some sugar cookies yesterday," she said, indicating several of them on a small platter.

"And you think I have a sweet tooth?" he asked with a faint smile as he sat down beside her on the sofa. He'd taken off his suit jacket and tie and rolled up the sleeves of his white linen shirt. He looked rakish with the top buttons of that shirt undone. She had to stifle a memory of opening them herself and touching him, kissing him, where the hair was thickest over those warm, firm muscles.

"You used to have one," she said finally.

"I'm partial to lemon...." He bit into one and chuckled. She'd used lemon flavoring. "Were you expecting me?" he asked.

She was outraged. "Of course not! I like lemon myself, so don't get arrogant, if you please."

"Oh, I've given up arrogance, Corrie. It got too damned expensive. Put cream into this coffee for me, will you? No sugar."

She complied. He couldn't do it himself, of course. He sat there in his lordly way watching her perform these menial tasks for him with the arrogance he said he'd forsaken. Fat chance!

She handed him the china cup and watched him balance it, in its saucer, on his broad, muscular thigh. She realized that she was staring and averted her attention to her own cup.

"Did you really bake the cookies?" he asked conversationally.

She nodded. "I've been studying cookbooks lately. I haven't made desserts in a long time. Dad was a borderline diabetic, remember? He wasn't supposed to have sweets and I didn't like to eat them in front of him."

"You can make these as often as you like," he murmured, finishing off another one. "They're good."

"Thanks." She nibbled on one without tasting it. "How's Sandy?"

"Missing you. So is Shep."

"She brought him to see me," she said.

"I know. He cries at night."

Her face stiffened. "When I get a place of my own, I'll bring him home."

"There's an easier way. Why don't *you* come home?"

She dropped her eyes. "The ranch isn't my home."

He finished his coffee and put the cup and saucer down on the table. Then he leaned back and slowly undid the rest of the buttons of his shirt, his eyes holding Coreen's relentlessly while he slid the fabric back from the thick salt-and-pepper hair that covered his broad chest.

Her lips parted as she tried to breathe normally. "Would you like some more coffee?" she asked a little breathlessly.

He shook his head slowly. He tugged the fabric out of his slacks and unfastened his belt. He slipped it out of the loops and tossed it to one side. Then he leaned back again, his legs splayed, and smiled at her with cool, dark arrogance. When he spoke, his voice was like velvet.

"Come here," he said.

Her eyes widened like saucers. Her heart began to run. It wasn't fair of him to taunt her this way, to invite her to make a fool of herself twice in one lifetime. Her lower lip trembled as she clamped down hard on her passion for him.

He began to smile, because he knew how hard it was for her to resist him. He'd always known.

"Afraid of me?" he taunted gently. "We'll go at your pace. I won't make you do anything you don't want to."

Her eyes burned with sudden tears as she remembered her own weakness, and what had followed it. "Are you having fun, Ted?" she asked, her voice choked. "Why don't you hit me and see if that feels as good as mocking me does?" She got up and started to leave the room.

He was faster. She'd barely gone two feet before he had her. She was caught and turned and held, her cheek against thick hair and damp muscle, the clean scent of him in her nostrils, the warmth of his body enveloping her.

"Don't cry," he whispered at her temple. His voice wasn't quite steady, and his hands were bruising against her back. "I'm not playing. Not this time."

"It will be just like it was before," she whispered brokenly, hitting him impotently with her fist. "You've hurt me enough . . . !"

His chest rose heavily under her cheek. "Yes. You, and myself. Now it all seems rather futile, although I meant well, at the time." He tilted her chin up so that he could see her ravaged face. "Take a good look, honey. I'm not a young man anymore."

"Did you ever notice how much younger Abby Ballenger is than Calhoun?" she asked solemnly.

He'd tried not to. The age difference between the long-married couple was pretty much the same as that between Ted and Coreen.

He frowned down at her. "Oh, yes," he said. "I've noticed."

"They have three sons," she reminded him. "And they've been married forever. Abby would die for Calhoun."

His jaw clenched. "No doubt he would for her, too."

Her eyes fell to his jutting chin and just above it to the long, firm lines of his mouth. The warm embrace was making her weak, just as being close to him always had. She wanted to crawl into his arms and stay there forever. But she had to remember that her time with him was limited to brief kisses that he always regretted and, somehow, made her pay for.

She let her eyes fall to his chest with a long sigh. "Isn't my time about up?" she asked.

"Up?"

"And by now, you should be feeling enough guilt to say something unpleasant and chase me away."

He grimaced as he stared over her head toward the wall beyond. "Is that what I do?"

"It used to seem like it."

He smoothed a lean hand over her hair and pressed her cheek closer to his bare flesh. The contact made his body ripple with pleasure. "I'll probably always feel a little guilt," he said deeply. "I could have spared you Barry."

"How? By sacrificing yourself in his place?" she asked with soft bitterness.

"It wouldn't have been a sacrifice." His mouth eased down to her forehead and pressed there softly, moving lazily to close both her eyes in turn. His warm hand cradled her cheek while his thumb moved over her lips. "Can you hear my heartbeat?" he whispered huskily.

"It's . . . very fast."

His hand moved down, slowly, over her breast to cup it tenderly. The heel of his palm pushed against her. "So is yours," he murmured. "Fast and hard."

She had no secrets from him now. Her trembling seemed to accelerate at their proximity.

"Come closer," he murmured as his mouth hovered over hers. "I want to feel your legs against mine."

"Isn't it . . . dangerous?" she whispered.

"Yes."

The tender amusement belied the threat. She moved forward a step and caught her breath at the feel of his body so intimately.

"Don't pull away," he said at her lips. "I don't mind if you know how aroused I am. It doesn't matter anymore."

Her hands spread out on his bare chest, and they tingled at the contact.

"Caress me," he said huskily, nibbling her lips. "Drive me mad."

She brushed her palms against him and looked up into eyes that darkened with pleasure. "Do you like it?"

"I like it." He nuzzled her nose with his, her mouth with his lips. The silence in the room was shattered by the sound of their ragged breathing. "I'd like it better if I could feel you with nothing between us."

She must be crazy. In fact, she was convinced of it when her hands went to the fastening at her back and slipped it while her mouth answered the teasing of his lips. She pushed up her T-shirt and suddenly felt her breasts starkly bare against the thick mat of hair that covered his damp skin.

"God!" he groaned, going rigid.

She stood very still, her wide eyes seeking his for reassurance.

His hands were tremulous on her face as he tilted it up to his blazing eyes. "Open your mouth." He bit off the words against her lips.

It was the last thing she understood in the turbulent minutes that followed. His hands, his mouth, the burning fever that no amount of contact seemed to quench made her mindless. His skin dragged against hers and she wept because she couldn't get close enough. She told him so in shaky whispers against his devouring mouth.

"There's only one way you and I will ever get close enough to each other," he said roughly. "And you know exactly what it is."

"Yes," she moaned. Her arms contracted around his bare back, her hands digging into the hard muscles of his shoulders. "Ted!"

He bent suddenly and lifted her into his arms. His eyes frightened her with their glitter. He hesitated, asking a question that he didn't have to put into words.

She buried her face in his throat and clung to him, shivering. Whatever he did now, it would be all right. If she had nothing else, she'd have now.

His arms shuddered as he stood there, feverish, aching for her.

"At least . . . make me pregnant," she whispered, anguished. "Give me that, if I can have nothing more."

The words shocked him. He looked down at the warm burden in his arms and felt them all the way to his heart. "Corrie!" he whispered.

Her eyes opened, dazed, helpless. "Is it really so shocking a thing to ask?" she asked miserably. "I know you don't want commitment. I won't ask anything of you, in case you're worried about that.''

He couldn't speak. He clasped her to his heart and rocked her, poleaxed, lost for words.

"Oh, Ted, don't you want a child?" she asked in a wobbly whisper. "I'd take ever such good care of him, or her. And you could come and visit when you wanted to..."

His eyes closed on a harsh groan, and for an instant his arms hurt her.

She bit her lower lip. He hadn't moved. Not a step. He just stood there holding her, cradling her. Probably feeling sorry for her as he realized the depths of her humiliation, she thought miserably. He didn't know what to do now.

She forced herself to breathe slowly, so that her pulse rate began to lessen a little. She didn't know how she was going to ever look him in the eye again. She'd humbled herself too far this time, gambled for stakes that suddenly seemed impossibly high. When would she ever learn?

"Please put me down now, Ted," she said with the little bit of dignity she retained.

His mouth slid over her wet eyes and closed them. He didn't put her down. He moved toward the armchair and slowly dropped down into it, cradling her like treasure.

"Ted?" she repeated.

His cheek rubbed against hers as he searched blindly for her mouth. It was wet. But she couldn't think anymore, because he was kissing her. It felt very much like desperation, so urgent that she felt the bruising pressure of his mouth and arms like a brand.

Her hand went up to his lean face and traced its line from the temple. She touched his closed eye and felt the moisture that drained from it. It took a minute to register, and then her eyes flew open and she pulled back from him.

His pale eyes were as wet as his cheek. He stared into hers without embarrassment, without subterfuge.

"Lie still," he said roughly. He dealt with the disheveled fabric that only half concealed her and tossed it carelessly onto the floor. His hand traced her bare breasts, lingering on the long scar across one, tenderly exploring her in a silence that blazed with hope.

He bent toward her and, with aching tenderness, drew his mouth over the length of the scar.

He nuzzled the hard nipple with his nose and then his mouth, testing its firmness until she gasped.

"Would it embarrass you to breast-feed a child?" he whispered then.

Hope flared through her like wildfire. "No!"

His mouth opened on her with gentle hunger. He arched her up to his ardent lips and held her there, in a bow. "I probably won't be as fertile as a young man," he said gruffly. "It may take longer."

She gasped, cradling his face to her. She trembled with joy as understanding dawned.

He buried his lips between her breasts and he kissed his way down to her waistline, where his mouth rested hungrily for a long time.

When he finally came up for air, he moved them both to the sofa, where he stretched out with an exhausted Corrie in his arms. His long legs tangled with hers intimately, casually, as if they'd lain together like this all their lives.

His head rested on a sofa pillow while hers lay over his heart and listened to its heavy, hard beat. Skin against skin, breath against breath. The intimacy was as exciting as it was unexpected.

"Why did you stop?" she asked drowsily.

His hand smoothed down her back to her waist. "We aren't going to make our first child until we're married," he said softly.

She stiffened. "But . . . but you said . . ."

He rolled her over onto her back and looked down into her wide, tender blue eyes hungrily. "I said that we could try to make a baby together," he whispered. "I didn't say that I wanted our child to be illegitimate."

"You don't want to get married."

He kissed away the quick tears, smiling with cynical self-reproach. "No, I don't," he agreed quietly. "I think you'll grow tired of me in time and wish you'd waited for a younger man to love. But I suppose I'll have to deal with that when the time comes."

She searched his beloved face with eyes that worshiped it. "You'll have a very long wait," she whispered. "I fell in love with you when I was barely twenty. I've loved you every day since. I'd give up my home, my self-respect, my honor . . . my very life for you."

Dark color burned along his cheekbones. "Corrie . . ."

"It's all right, Ted. I know that you don't feel that way about me," she continued with quiet dignity. "But maybe after the children are born and you grow to love them, you'll be happy."

He was so choked with feeling that he could hardly speak. He touched her soft mouth lightly, searching for words. "It's so damned hard for me," he began.

She put her fingers over his mouth with a soft sigh. "You don't have to say a thing."

His pale eyes slid down her body and she winced.

"I'm sorry about the scar," she said, looking at it. "Maybe it will fade."

"Do you think I care?" he ground out.

She winced again at his tone. "Ted . . ."

"Your breasts are perfect," he said flatly. "Scar or no scar. You're perfect to me. You always have been. Always!"

She didn't know how to answer that.

He ran a rough hand through his damp hair, looked down at her and groaned. "I can't handle any more of this without doing something about it," he said huskily, and rolled away from her.

He got to his feet, walking away to the kitchen. He came back minutes later with a fresh pot of coffee. By then, Corrie had her clothing back in its former order and was trying not to meet his eyes.

He poured coffee, aware of her shy glances at his broad, bare chest.

"Like what you see?" he chided gently.

She glared at him. "You don't have to gloat."

"Sure I do." He chuckled. "It isn't every day that a woman offers herself up like a living sacrifice. Isn't that what they used to do with virgins in primitive times—offer them to some frightening monster as a deterrent?"

"You're not a monster," she returned, lifting her coffee to her mouth. "And I'm not afraid of you."

"I noticed," he said dryly. He leaned back, sliding an affectionate arm around her shoulders to draw her to his chest again. He lifted his legs onto the coffee table and crossed them lazily. "Where do you want to be married?"

Her eyes darted up to his face. "Are you sure?"

He nodded. "Where?"

"Jacobsville, then. And Sandy can be maid of honor."

"Since you're so keen on the Ballengers, I'll ask Calhoun to be best man."

She didn't know if he was being sarcastic, but it sounded that way. She was quiet.

He tilted her chin. "You're like an open book to me," he said solemnly. "I wasn't trying to sound cynical. Did I?"

She nodded.

He sighed. "You'll get used to me. A lot of times I say things in the heat of the moment that I don't really mean. I lose my temper sometimes when I shouldn't. I'm set in my ways."

"I know."

He lifted an eyebrow. "Second thoughts, Corrie?"

She stared into her coffee cup. "I want to have your baby," she whispered. "Ted, for heaven's... sake...!"

The coffee had gone everywhere, as if his hand had suddenly developed a huge spring. He muttered apologies and started grabbing for paper napkins to mop them both up.

"Don't say things like that to me when I've got a cupful of hot coffee, for God's sake!" he raged, glaring at her from his superior height. "Don't you know that it's taking every ounce of willpower I've got to sit here calmly with you when all I want to do is get you into the nearest bed!"

Chapter Eleven

Coreen flushed wildly at the stark exclamation. "Well, you don't have to make it sound like some sinful orgy, do you?"

"That's what it is," he returned. "Sinful. Dangerous. Delicious. Forbidden."

"You want it, too," she accused.

"I want you," he said heavily. "You! It never stops." His eyes betrayed him, for once. "It never has and it never will."

The confession made her breathless. She sat down, ignoring the coffee stains on the sofa, and stared up at him helplessly.

"Why don't you laugh?" he demanded. "Don't you feel entitled to rub my nose in it? I've given you enough hell over the years that you should feel vengeful."

"All I feel is hungry," she whispered. "I love you so

much, Ted," she added on a shaky breath. "More than you could imagine in your wildest dreams."

His face went hard. "Prove it. Marry me tomorrow."

"Tomorrow," she agreed huskily.

"No protests? No postponements?"

She shook her head.

He nodded slowly. "All right."

He left five minutes later. The next morning they were married by a nervous justice of the peace in Jacobsville, with a shocked and delighted Sandy for maid of honor and a highly amused Calhoun and Abby Ballenger for witnesses.

After the ceremony, everyone congratulated her and then Ted, and walked out arm in arm, speaking in incredulous whispers.

"Shell-shock," Ted informed Coreen when they were back at the Victoria apartment two hours later. "They think I've lost my mind."

"So do I," she agreed.

He turned, his pale eyes possessive on his new wife in her neat white suit and pale pink blouse. There had been a pillbox hat with the ensemble and a white veil over it. Ted had lifted the veil to kiss her with brief affection in the justice of the peace's office.

"I want you," he said roughly. "Right now."

She flushed. She'd thought they might have a meal, go to a movie, do something together. Apparently this was his idea of togetherness, and perhaps the only sort he wanted with her.

"All . . . all right," she said, taken aback.

He shepherded her into the bedroom, closed and locked the door and took the phone off the hook. It wasn't even dark, and she was intimidated by the passion in his eyes and the urgency of his hands on her clothing.

"I won't hurt you," he said unevenly as he divested her of jacket, blouse and skirt in short order. "I swear to God I won't. Just . . . bear with me, if you can."

"Of course," she said nervously.

He slid the rest of her clothing from her stiff body and lifted her gently onto the bed. His pale eyes wandered over her like loving hands, lingering, possessing until a muffled groan broke from his tight lips.

He sat down and pulled off his boots. Coreen turned her head away while he undressed, dreading her own inability to respond so quickly to him.

Scant minutes later, he pulled her into his arms and she felt the impact of his nudity against her like a long, hot brand. She gasped.

He broke her mouth open under his, and his hands began to smooth over her back in long, slow caresses. She felt his arousal against her smooth belly and stiffened.

"Open your eyes," he said huskily. "Watch me while I take you."

She flushed as she complied, her embarrassment plain in the eyes that watched him lever above her.

He coaxed her legs apart and eased between them. She felt him in total intimacy and was shocked into looking down. Her eyes widened and her body went rigid.

"So that's what you think," he murmured gently, and smiled. He chuckled as he settled himself against her and relaxed. "No," he said. "Not quick. Not this time. I only want you to get used to the feel of me. But you'll beg me before you get me."

She didn't understand. Not then. But fraught minutes later, after his mouth had explored every silken inch of her and then his hands had kindled sensations that had to be sinful because of their incredible stimulation, she did understand.

She was perspiring madly, shivering all over with a throbbing ache in her lower body that was new and frightening. And he kept the intimate contact between them, but when she lifted her hips to coax him into possession, he lifted free of her tempting pressure.

By the third time it happened, she was in tears. "Oh...please," she sobbed, lifting to him in such a tense arch that her whole body shuddered with the strain. "Oh, please, it aches...so!"

"Aches," he agreed huskily. "Burns. Throbs like a wound." His lean hand slid up her thigh and caught it firmly. "Look, Corrie. Look!"

He pulled her up toward the hovering threat of his masculinity and slowly, tortuously, let his body ease into hers.

She gasped, shivering, at the feel of him. She was so aroused that the tiny hesitation her body caused him was only part of the miracle. She looked down and her eyes dilated feverishly as she saw them join.

Her rose flush mirrored his own fascination. None of his experiences had prepared him for the shock of her virginity, or its implications. He was her first lover. In spite of everything, he was the first.

His fingers dug into her soft thigh and he caught his breath. "My God," he whispered, awed.

Her own eyes sought his then, wet with tears, wide with wonder.

His teeth clenched at the hot wave of pleasure that shot through him as he felt her take him completely. He met her eyes for a second before he groaned and lost control.

She felt the impact of his weight on her as he pressed her hungrily into the mattress, his hands under her hips, his muscular body suddenly dancing with hers in a rhythm that she felt to the soles of her feet.

"Match me," he whispered urgently into her mouth. "Yes...yes! Take me...take all of me....take me, Corrie!"

She cried out as the deep, dragging pleasure suddenly spread over her like fire, throbbing, throbbing, throbbing!

He groaned harshly and his breath raked his throat as he gave in to the same madness that had her in its sweet grip. For endless, aching seconds, they shared the same soul.

His forehead was damp against her breasts. She felt her heartbeat, like an unsprung watch, shaking him in her clasping arms.

"I couldn't have waited one more minute," he whispered harshly. "Years of waiting, years of holding you in my arms, only to wake at dawn and find you gone!" His arms tightened and his mouth moved hungrily against her body. "I've got you now. You're mine, and I'll never let you go!"

Coreen heard him, but it took a minute for the words to register. "Years?"

"Years." He nuzzled his face against her soft breast. "Corrie, I haven't had a woman in almost three years," he said heavily.

She went very still in his arms. "But...but all those photos in the gossip columns!"

"Window dressing," he murmured with a harsh laugh. "I couldn't even feel desire for anyone else. You were all I wanted. Only you, Corrie."

"But you let me marry Barry! You said...you said you didn't want me!"

His arms contracted. "I tried so hard to be noble," he said, his voice tormented. "I wanted to spare you a husband so much older than you, whom you might regret marrying one day, don't you see? I had no idea, none at all, what a hell Barry would make of your life! I have even that on my conscience." His voice went husky. "I loved you. Loved you more than honor. More than self-respect. More than my life."

Her own words. Echoed. Felt. She closed her eyes and tears slid from them, burning her cheeks. She began to sob.

Vaguely she heard him gasp, felt his mouth taking away the tears, soothing away the pain. He eased over her, his body as gentle as his mouth, loving her with motions as tender as they were stimulating. Possessing her all over again, but with such love that she wept all through it, until the contractions began deep in her body and echoed in his, until they lay as close as two souls, straining together in the soft explosion of ecstasy that formed total communion.

He didn't move away afterward. He held her to him while he rolled over onto his back, sparing her his weight. But they were still joined, completely.

He drew in a shaken breath, feeling her so much a part of him that when he breathed, her body moved with him.

"It will be like this every time, now, when we love," he said deeply, smoothing her back with lean, tender hands.

She smiled and kissed his damp chest. "When we love," she echoed shakily. Her hands clung to him. "Don't ever let go."

His arms enfolded her and he smiled with loving exhaustion. "Well . . . maybe just long enough to eat," he murmured dryly. "Eventually."

Sandy glowered at both of them when they told her, six weeks later, that she was going to be an aunt.

"It's positively indecent," she muttered. "You've only been married six weeks today!"

Ted managed to look proud and sheepish all at once, his hand tight around Coreen's as she looked up at him with pure adoration.

"We're in a hurry," he said.

"No kidding!" Sandy said sarcastically.

"I'm not getting any younger," he continued, but without any traces of resentment or bitterness.

"And we did have in mind a baseball team," Coreen lied, tongue-in-cheek.

Sandy burst out laughing and hugged them both. "Well, I'm very happy," she confessed. "But what are people going to say?"

Actually they said very little. Mostly they grinned at the inseparable newlyweds who were so obviously in love and offered double congratulations.

As Ted later told his beaming wife, it was mostly his pride that had kept him from proposing to her years ago. Now Regan's pride was his wife—and the child they would both welcome.

*   *   *   *   *

HE'S MORE THAN A MAN,
HE'S ONE OF OUR

Fabulous Fathers

MIRACLE DAD
by Toni Collins

Single father Derek Wolfe didn't think a miracle was too much to ask for when it came to his children's happiness. But when he demanded to leave heaven and return to them, he never considered the consequences. His children didn't recognize him, and their guardian, Evelyn Sloan, thought Derek was her fiancé! Derek found himself in an earthly dilemma—he could step in as father to his children again *only* if he married Evelyn....

Available in May from Silhouette Romance

Fall in love with our FABULOUS FATHERS!

Silhouette
R O M A N C E™

MILLION DOLLAR SWEEPSTAKES (III)
AND
EXTRA BONUS PRIZE DRAWING

No purchase necessary. To enter both prize offers and receive the Free Books and Surprise Gift, follow the directions published and complete and mail your "Match 3" Game Card. If not taking advantage of the book and gift offer or if the "Match 3" Game Card is missing, you may enter by hand-printing your name and address on a 3" X 5" card and mailing it (limit: one entry per envelope) via First Class Mail to: Million Dollar Sweepstakes (III) "Match 3" Game, P.O. Box 1867, Buffalo, NY 14269-1867, or Million Dollar Sweepstakes (III) "Match 3" Game, P.O. Box 609, Fort Erie, Ontario L2A 5X3. When your entry is received, you will be assigned Million Dollar Sweepstakes (III) numbers and be entered in the Extra Bonus Prize Drawing. To be eligible entries must be received no later than March 31, 1996. No liability is assumed for printing errors or lost, late or misdirected entries. Odds of winning are determined by the number of eligible entries distributed and received.

Sweepstakes open to residents of the U.S. (except Puerto Rico), Canada, Europe and Taiwan who are 18 years of age or older. All applicable laws and regulations apply. Sweepstakes offers void wherever prohibited by law. Values of all prizes are in U.S. currency. This sweepstakes is presented by Torstar Corp, its subsidiaries and affiliates, in conjunction with book, merchandise and/or product offerings. For a copy of the official rules of the Million Dollar Sweepstakes (III), send a self-addressed, stamped envelope (WA residents need not affix return postage) to: MILLION DOLLAR SWEEPSTAKES (III) Rules, P.O. Box 4573, Blair, NE 68009, USA; for a copy of the Extra Bonus Prize Drawing rules, send a self-addressed, stamped envelope (WA residents need not affix return postage) to: Extra Bonus Prize Drawing Rules, P.O. Box 4590, Blair, NE 68009, USA.

SWP-S494

It's our 1000th Silhouette Romance™, and we're celebrating!

And to say "THANK YOU" to our wonderful readers, we would like to send you a

FREE AUSTRIAN CRYSTAL BRACELET

This special bracelet truly captures the spirit of CELEBRATION 1000! and is a stunning complement to any outfit! And it can be yours FREE just for enjoying SILHOUETTE ROMANCE™.

FREE GIFT OFFER

To receive your free gift, complete the certificate according to directions. Be certain to enclose the required number of proofs-of-purchase. Requests must be received no later than August 31, 1994. Please allow 6 to 8 weeks for receipt of order. Offer good while quantities of gifts last. Offer good in U.S. and Canada only.

And that's not all! Readers can also enter our...

CELEBRATION 1000! SWEEPSTAKES

In honor of our 1000th SILHOUETTE ROMANCE™, we'd like to award $1000 to a lucky reader!

As an added value every time you send in a completed offer certificate with the correct amount of proofs-of-purchase, your name will automatically be entered in our CELEBRATION 1000! Sweepstakes. The sweepstakes features a grand prize of $1000. PLUS, 1000 runner-up prizes of a FREE SILHOUETTE ROMANCE™, autographed by one of CELEBRATION 1000!'s special featured authors will be awarded. These volumes are sure to be cherished for years to come, a true commemorative keepsake.

DON'T MISS YOUR OPPORTUNITY TO WIN! ENTER NOW!

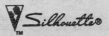

CELOFFER

IT'S OUR 1000TH SILHOUETTE ROMANCE, AND WE'RE CELEBRATING!

JOIN US FOR A SPECIAL COLLECTION OF LOVE STORIES
BY AUTHORS YOU'VE LOVED FOR YEARS, AND
NEW FAVORITES YOU'VE JUST DISCOVERED.
JOIN THE CELEBRATION...

April
REGAN'S PRIDE by **Diana Palmer**
MARRY ME AGAIN by **Suzanne Carey**

May
THE BEST IS YET TO BE by **Tracy Sinclair**
CAUTION: BABY AHEAD by **Marie Ferrarella**

June
THE BACHELOR PRINCE by **Debbie Macomber**
A ROGUE'S HEART by **Laurie Paige**

July
IMPROMPTU BRIDE by **Annette Broadrick**
THE FORGOTTEN HUSBAND by **Elizabeth August**

SILHOUETTE ROMANCE...VIBRANT, FUN AND EMOTIONALLY
RICH! TAKE ANOTHER LOOK AT US! AND AS PART OF THE
CELEBRATION, READERS CAN RECEIVE A FREE GIFT!

YOU'LL FALL IN LOVE ALL OVER AGAIN WITH SILHOUETTE ROMANCE!

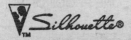

CELEBRATION 1000! Free Gift Offer

ORDER INFORMATION:

To receive your free AUSTRIAN CRYSTAL BRACELET, send three original proof-of-purchase coupons from any SILHOUETTE ROMANCE™ title published in April through July 1994 with the Free Gift Certificate completed, plus $1.75 for postage and handling (check or money order—please do not send cash) payable to Silhouette Books CELEBRATION 1000! Offer. Hurry! Quantities are limited.

FREE GIFT CERTIFICATE   096 KBM

Name:_____

Address:_____

City:_____ State/Prov.:_____ Zip/Postal:_____

Mail this certificate, three proofs-of-purchase and check or money order to CELEBRATION 1000! Offer, Silhouette Books, 3010 Walden Avenue, P.O. Box 9057, Buffalo, NY 14269-9057 or P.O. Box 622, Fort Erie, Ontario L2A 5X3. Please allow 4-6 weeks for delivery. Offer expires August 31, 1994.

PLUS

Every time you submit a completed certificate with the correct number of proofs-of-purchase, you are automatically entered in our CELEBRATION 1000! SWEEPSTAKES to win the GRAND PRIZE of $1000 CASH! PLUS, 1000 runner-up prizes of a FREE Silhouette Romance™, autographed by one of CELEBRATION 1000!'s special featured authors, will be awarded. No purchase or obligation necessary to enter. See below for alternate means of entry and how to obtain complete sweepstakes rules.

CELEBRATION 1000! SWEEPSTAKES
NO PURCHASE OR OBLIGATION NECESSARY TO ENTER

You may enter the sweepstakes without taking advantage of the CELEBRATION 1000! FREE GIFT OFFER by hand-printing on a 3" x 5" card (mechanical reproductions are not acceptable) your name and address and mailing it to: CELEBRATION 1000! Sweepstakes, P.O. Box 9057, Buffalo, NY 14269-9057 or P.O. Box 622, Fort Erie, Ontario L2A 5X3. Limit: one entry per envelope. Entries must be sent via First Class mail and be received no later than August 31, 1994. No liability is assumed for lost, late or misdirected mail.

Sweepstakes is open to residents of the U.S. (except Puerto Rico) and Canada, 18 years of age or older. All federal, state, provincial, municipal and local laws apply. Offer void wherever prohibited by law. Odds of winning dependent on the number of entries received. For complete rules, send a self-addressed, stamped envelope to: CELEBRATION 1000! Rules, P.O. Box 4200, Blair, NE 68009.

 ## ONE PROOF OF PURCHASE

096KBM

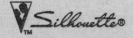